SCENE 75

a novel

RAHI MASOOM RAZA

SCENE 75

a novel

Translated by

Poonam Saxena

HARPER PERENNIAL

NEWYORK • LONDON • TORONTO • SYDNEY • NEW DELHI

First published in India in 2017 by Harper Perennial
An imprint of HarperCollins *Publishers*

HarperCollins Publishers India, Cyber City, Building 10-A, Gurugram,
Haryana-122002, India
www.harpercollins.co.in

2 4 6 8 10 9 7 5 3 1

First published in Hindi in 1977 by Rajkamal Prakashan, Delhi

P-ISBN: 978-93-5277-042-7
E-ISBN: 978-93-5277-043-4

Typeset in 12/17.2 Apollo MT Std
by Saanvi Graphics, Noida

Printed and bound at
MicroPrints India, New Delhi

MIX
Paper
FSC FSC™ C218906

This product is made of FSC®-certified and other controlled material.

HarperCollins Publishers, Macken House, 39/40 Mayor Street
Upper, Dublin 1, D01 C9W8, Ireland

Will and Testament

My art is dead, my friends
My skin has turned blue, my friends
Take me to the Ganga in Ghazipur, let me sleep in
her lap.
But it could be that I die far from my homeland
So this is my will
If a little river flows in that foreign city
Take me there
Let me sleep in her lap
And tell her
That this son of the Ganga is now hers.

I am the son of three mothers. Nafisa Begum, Aligarh University, and the Ganga. I gift *Scene: 75* to them. Nafisa Begum is dead. I can't remember her very clearly. But the other two mothers are alive and I remember them well.

– Rahi Masoom Raza

Preface

Whoever you see,
Whoever you meet,
They seem like someone else.
In this neighbourhood
It's as if no one has an identity.

On the stairs
Once again, the sound of someone's footsteps.
Once again, someone without a face,
Gilt-tongued, stone-hearted.
He will come,
And smiling,
Take away a sliver of my heart.

– Rahi Masoom Raza

Fade In

BEYOND THE bars of the window, on the other side of the grille, the moon had descended and paused at the cluster of coconut trees, and Ali Amjad, his face pressed against the bars, was gazing at this moon sinking amidst the coconuts. It wasn't clear whether Ali Amjad was trapped inside the room or whether the moon was trapped outside it.

Perhaps they both were imprisoned. One inside and the other outside. The moon was lifeless, and for a few days now, Ali Amjad too had stopped counting himself among the living, and perhaps that's why, for a few days now, he had taken a liking to the moon.

The room was filled with the silence of the night. Outside the room too, there was a deep nocturnal silence. The cluster of coconut trees was silent. The old ruined fort was silent. The road that embraced the crumbling ruin and, for no reason, suddenly stopped at a bay, now bereft of fishermen's boats festooned with green, yellow, saffron and tricoloured flags, too was silent. The bay had undoubtedly been important or useful once, otherwise why would a fort have been built right at its mouth? Boats must have sailed down that bay, and that's why a rough, makeshift road must have been built, which some corporation in newly independent India had then coated with tar and concrete, making it a respectable, proper road. And once that road became respectable and proper for no reason, it became necessary to give it a name. So after having lived in anonymity for a couple of hundred years, all of a sudden, the road acquired a name. A big cement board was erected and the words 'Lala Asharfilal Marg' were written on it in Roman, Devanagari and Marathi scripts. A deputy minister inaugurated the road and immediately afterwards, everyone – the deputy minister and all the people who lived on that road – promptly forgot its name, and the sturdy column supporting the grand cement board was used only by dogs to pee on.

No one asked the corporation why the road had been given a name, nor did anyone ask who Lala Asharfilal was. The make-up and naming of the road had cost three lakh twenty-seven thousand eight hundred and sixteen rupees and four and a quarter annas – annas, because this event occurred at a time when the naya paisa had not yet come into use and all transactions were carried out in annas and pice, even though young people of that generation didn't know what a pice looked like. Students had only heard that something called 'pice' existed and was useful in matters of accounting and commerce. Four pice made one paisa. Four paise made one anna. Four annas made one chavanni. Two chavannis made one atthanni. Two atthannis made one rupee. Between the chavanni and the anna was a duanni. There was even an adhanni between an anna and a paisa. It was lots of fun, doing accounts in those days. You had to climb up a ladder to go from a pice to a rupee. But when the naya paisa and rupee were introduced, the rungs of the ladder vanished and doing accounts was robbed of all enjoyment. Rich moneylenders took advantage of this. By the time people began to understand the naya paisa-rupee system, prices had already shot up sky high and every Damdilal became a Lala Asharfilal. And only when the Lala – after whom our road was named – died because his heart stopped beating, did the whole country realize for the first time that the Lalaji actually had a heart in his breast. Magazines and newspapers had a field day. One journalist wrote that when Allah had fashioned Asharfilal's likeness, the supply room sent a message that it had run out of hearts. But the likeness was ready. The bill had been raised. The delivery date had been finalized. That's when Allah mian took a silver coin with Queen Victoria's face on it, and put it inside Lala Asharfilal instead of a heart. Thus, Lala Asharfilal was ready to be dispatched. And that's why whatever he touched turned into money. But this didn't mean that Lalaji had installed a money-making machine in his house. Oh no. Lalaji was not that kind of man. He was a deeply religious personage. He did not discriminate on the basis of caste, religion or untouchability. Whether it was a Harijan or a Brahmin, he was impartial in extracting interest on loans, bringing lawsuits upon them, or confiscating and impounding their assets. He was the one who had borne the cost of erecting the elegant, shimmering Bharat Mata temple in the Chamartoli neighbourhood of his village Maharajganj. The Momin Ansar National Higher Secondary School in his city, that too was built on land he had donated.

He also constructed many shelters, for cows and for humans. And on days when it was difficult to procure sugar even for weddings, Lala Asharfilal made sure his Maharajganj ants were still fed their daily dose. It is said that after Lalaji died, swarming circles of ants waited for him on those paths for months...

Lalaji made a lot of money in the Second World War. He got many army tenders. And from an ordinary man, he turned into a Big Man. But soon he realized that nothing was going to stop India from becoming independent, and that Gandhi's party was going to rule the new nation. So, like many prominent nationalists, he cut off all ties with the British. He returned the title of Rai Sahib they'd conferred upon him, and went to jail. And when he was released after four months and twelve days of imprisonment, on 13 December 1945, he was counted among the patriots. In the 1952 elections, his older son became an MP, his younger son an MLA, and he himself passed away.

The nation was newly independent. Immediately after independence there was a sudden increase in the number of Big Men, but no significant increase in the number of roads. The result was that there weren't enough roads for all the Big Men. So every road was given two or three names. If, from this crossing to the next, the road was called Maulana Abdul Khaliq Marg, from that crossing to the next, it was called Babu Damdiprasad Marg. The road that used to be known as Clive Road became Netaji Subhash Chandra Bose Marg one fine day, as if there was no difference between the paths taken by Lord Clive and Subhash Chandra Bose…

But even changing the names of roads or giving one road many different names didn't solve the problem. The names of many important people were still left out. So, to accommodate all these other names, schools and colleges were opened. What we understand as the Education Development Programme was actually a Name Consumption Programme, and that's why the people appointed to teach in these schools and colleges were those who were considered unacceptable for any other work by the government and society.

Lala Asharfilal's sons, both the older and the younger one, were advised that they should take advantage of the situation and open a Lala Asharfilal Memorial National Degree College, and appoint their brother-in-law as its principal. It so happened that while the two brothers had separate wives, they had the same brother-in-law. And both the wives and the sole brother-in-law exerted their combined pressure on the two brothers to open a degree college. They explained the benefits of education to them. However, the brothers stubbornly insisted that they wanted a road. But there was no road left in all of India … With great difficulty, they found a dirt road of just three furlongs which ended abruptly at a nameless creek. Intensely relieved at the discovery, they decided to offload Lalaji there. But not before the road was made pukka and a deputy minister from Uttar Pradesh came to inaugurate it. It doesn't need to be pointed out that this deputy minister was the same, one and only, brother-in-law of the two brothers, who was supposed to become the principal of the degree college and thus get some gainful employment. But it turned out that he had become successful in politics. And if he hadn't been killed in a car accident, he might have gone on to become the chief minister of Uttar Pradesh … An editorial in an Opposition weekly declared that Uttar Pradesh would never forget this good turn Yamraj, the god of death, had done them.

If Lala Asharfilal had not been an important man, or if he had been but his two sons hadn't been an MP and an MLA respectively, or if his sons had been an MP and an MLA respectively but their brother-in-law hadn't been a deputy minister, and if *his* brother-in-law in turn hadn't been an important social worker in Bombay, the road would never have been named Lala Asharfilal Marg. And if the road hadn't been named Lala Asharfilal Marg, cooperative housing societies wouldn't have constructed buildings along it, and if these buildings had not been made, Ali Amjad would not have been gazing at the moon trapped in the cluster of coconut trees, engulfed by the quicksand of that silent, deserted night.

What all this proved was that time is a series of 'ifs' and there is a noose of many such 'ifs' around every neck. If only life didn't have this 'if' sticking to it like a tail, it would be so pleasant ... But there is no way to escape these 'ifs' in life.

Like many people, I mean many respectable people, Ali Amjad was both a believer in chance and in an ideal life not based on chance. When he exhibited fear he became the former, and if he felt anger at that fear he became the latter. And between this fear and this anger lay his entire life.

Ali Amjad was a middle-class man. And like all middle-class people, he was discontented. He was not so brave that he could win a Mahavir Chakra, nor was he such a coward that he didn't know how to fight. He was from Benares, where his grandfather had built a three-storey stone house in a dark alley in Govindpura Kalan. These small, many-storeyed houses of Benares had iron grilles over the courtyards so that the afternoon sun could trickle through. The lack of sunlight and fresh air meant that individuals could not flourish, and that's why Benares hasn't been able to produce a bigger political leader than Sampurnanand, or a greater physician than Hakim Kazim, or a greater poet than Nazeer Banarasi. And that's why the city has remained famous only for its temples, ghats, tawaifs, Kachori Gali, Kanthe Maharaj, Bismillah Khan, Sitara Devi, and out-of-control bulls.

Benares!

God knows where, and how, Benares is today.

Ali Amjad moved away from the window. After all, who can win a staring contest with the moon? The past, present and future might all blink, but the moon's steadfast gaze never falters. And what was Ali Amjad in comparison to the moon? His eyes, anyway, were prone to blinking. He had, anyway, more or less failed to meet his own gaze.

He looked at the moon once again. It was where it had been. Outside the room, the moonlit night was coming alive, and inside the room was an unnamed, sinister darkness. The pen lying on the table was awake.

I sold myself for the sake of ink.
So that a dry pen could not be
My reason for not writing.
I was compelled to write.
Helpless.
Crippled.
Powerless.

And the calendar on the wall was awake. 5 January. 1976. Sunday. 5 January. Oh god, it must be so cold there. Even the wind must be trying to escape the winter by burrowing into warm quilts. Now that cold was just a memory. A very warm memory. As if the doorbell would ring at that very moment, and the cold would race inside as soon as the door opened and wrap itself around him … Ali Amjad reached out and changed the date on the calendar. Instead of 5 January it became 6 January. Instead of Sunday it became Monday. Oh god! What a calamity! It was the day of the shoot. A nine o'clock shift. The scene wasn't ready and the needle on his wristwatch was nibbling away at time like a little mouse. It was twenty-seven minutes and twenty-five … twenty-six seconds past two … And the file lying open on the table was awake.

SCENE: 75: DAY: POST OFFICE

He had written this heading on the page at 8.30 in the evening. For the fourth time the director, Harish Rai, had said with some irritation: 'It's incredible, Amjad! You can't understand such a simple scene.'

The scene really was very simple. A munshi is sitting by the road, writing a letter, and an old lady is getting the letter written. Leela Mishra is playing the old woman, and Sanjeev Kumar is playing the street munshi.

But he really couldn't understand 'Scene: 75: Day: Post Office'. And Harish Rai was not wrong in asking him why he couldn't understand it, because were there any scenes in commercial Hindi cinema that one couldn't understand?

Premchand!

Yashpal!

Ali Abbas Husaini!

Rajinder Singh Bedi!

Krishan Chander!

Ismat Chughtai…

And in the room, all these names were awake.

The film's title was *Chaurahe ka Dada*. By now he was used to writing without thinking. Writing scenes was the easiest thing. Earlier when he thought and wrote, the director, the hero, the heroine, established character artists, everyone would start picking faults with the scenes, because everyone in the film world is a writer except for the writer himself. Never mind if they can't even speak proper Hindi, they are all writers. From Dilip Kumar to Raaj Kumar, everyone loves to write. Raaj Kumar, Rajesh Khanna, Dharmendra, Dilip Kumar ... everyone's homes are full of good books. Indeed, many people are able to make ends meet simply by supplying them books. But these poor stars, working three shifts a day, how can they find the time to read? As for writing, how much time does *that* take? Just take the writer's pen and 'fix' the scene...

At first, Ali Amjad didn't like this business of 'fixing' scenes at all. He would start arguing and fighting. And he would remain unemployed, lying around aimlessly in his guest house.

D'Cruz Guest House.

At the corner of Bandra Talao.

SCENE: 75

Four men ... Four dream merchants lived there together. There was a bed in one room. A sofa with torn upholstery which had been bought from a junk shop. Five pairs of trousers. Six shirts. Countless bedbugs. And four men.

Ali Amjad.

Harish Rai.

VD. (His name was Virendra Kumar. Once he 'happened' to you, you could never get rid of him, which is why he came to be known as VD.)

Alimullah Khan.

Ali Amjad had come to Bombay to become a writer. The way film as a medium was getting raped! India is an uncivilized country. And for uncivilized people, there is no medium more powerful than film. Krishan Chander, Bedi, Ismat aapa had brought shame to writers. Damn Shailendra, Majrooh and Sahir ... *'Laal laal gaal'* ... Wah! What poetry! These people have sold themselves for black money. They have lost their character and their ideals ... I won't do that ... me, me and me...

Even after staying in D'Cruz Guest House's mosquito- and bedbug-infested room for eight months or perhaps eight years or perhaps eight centuries, here he was, crucifying his dreams, Ali Amjad Naqvi, MA, LLB.

The four had decided amongst themselves that whoever arrived at the room first would get to sleep on the bed with the mosquito net. There was a story behind that bed. It had been made for a film titled *Adle-Jahangir* and was supposed to be the emperor Jahangir's bed. The day it arrived on the set, Jahangir broke his leg. The shoot was stalled for three months. When Jahangir's leg healed, Noorjehan got married and took off to Europe for her honeymoon. Nothing could be shot for two more months. By the time the dates were worked out all over again, Noorjehan had got divorced and gone off to Kashmir with an upcoming star to drown her sorrows, and there, in an inebriated state, she declared that this upcoming star was far more suited to playing Jahangir than that five-foot-five-inch actor. How could *he* play Jahangir! Whereupon Jahangir demanded that the heroine be changed. Another couple of months went by. The heroine was changed. The set was erected all over again. The day the shooting was to begin, a baby girl was born to the hero. His mood soured. The crew was asked to pack up. Now the producer became worried. What was happening? Cars ran to Burmawali, the famed seer of Worli. It was discovered that everything was the bed's fault ...

Harish Rai was the fourth assistant on that unit. He asked if he could keep that royal bed.

So, in truth, the bed belonged to Harish Rai. But all four of them were Leftists. Socialism, Che Guevara, Kanu Sanyal ... they thought and talked about them until late into the night, as they smoked their Charminar cigarettes. So how could any one man have sole rights to the bed? If they could turn four pairs of trousers into sixteen, how could one bed remain just one bed? Whoever came first would claim it.

Ali Amjad had landed some work at the time. He was writing stories for Phandaji. Phandaji was very secular but didn't eat anything that had been touched by a Muslim, so Harish Rai had introduced Ali Amjad as Gaurishankar Lal 'Krantikari'. Apart from writing stories, Ali Amjad also had to rewrite Phandaji's daughter Pushplata's poems, and listen to Phanda Patialvi's eyewitness accounts of the treachery of Muslims. Though when the riots were actually taking place in Peshawar, Rawalpindi and Lahore, Phandaji was in Bareilly selling medicines. Years later, when he discovered that Gaurishankar Lal 'Krantikari' was actually Ali Amjad, he stopped talking to him. And as for Harish Rai, Phandaji didn't want to look at his face again. In those days he was quite influential, so poor Harish Rai was thrown out of many projects ... But now, because of this wretched 'Scene: 75: Day: Post Office', he had to hassle his friend. *Chaurahe ka Dada* was Harish's first big film. Harish had every right to throw a tantrum.

He picked his pen up as if it were a sword, and sat down. He'd fix this damned scene! He began writing:

> The scene begins with the munshi sitting by the road, one leg folded under him, the other raised and bent at the knee. Across his knee lies a writing board upon which he is writing a letter. The stitching of his pyjamas is frayed at the crotch.

He stopped. He ran his pen across the last sentence. For one, the women on the Censor Board would not allow the stitching to be frayed at the crotch and, second, the financier and his family would be annoyed by the idea and want to know why the munshi's pyjamas must be torn. The heroine had been paid four and a half lakhs. Now if the stitching of *her* clothes came undone, at least it would please the fucking public! And if then the censors chopped it off, it would make no difference...

God knows why, he suddenly remembered Mrs D'Souza from Mai's Adda. VD had found out about this adda in the days when they were always broke. Mr D'Souza was a junior excise inspector, and Mai's Adda fell in his area, so he used to take a cut from the earnings.

They said that Mai had been quite a woman in her time. Despite being a woman, she could teach men a thing or two about cursing. The big bosses of Danda called her 'Mai' and came to her to pay their respects. Even the cops began calling her 'Mai'. She was a vegetarian, but no one could match her when it came to frying fish. The alcohol at her adda was far superior to what you would find at other such establishments – no wonder Mai's Adda was so popular among film folk. From Raj Kapoor to Sahir Ludhianvi, everyone had drunk on credit there. She only gave credit to people from the film industry – she had a special relationship with them. Her son Shyamlal Banarasi worked as an extra in films. He was such a fine-looking young man that all the heroines were crazy about him. But he didn't so much as raise his eyes to look at them. During the day, he would happily work in films and then, until late at night, he would work at the adda. But suddenly, god knows what got into him, he decided to start a union for extras. 'The suppliers eat up all our money,' he said. 'They harass our sister extras. We will make a union. Inquilab zindabad!' One day, when he was returning from a meeting at Famous Studios in Mahalaxmi, someone stabbed him in the back with a knife ... So he became a real martyr for the film industry, didn't he! Whenever one of her debtors became famous, Mai would hang his photograph in her adda and talk about him as if he were her own son ... No one had ever seen Mai cry, but after Shyamlal's death she aged overnight. Around the same time, Mr D'Souza retired and bought over Mai's Adda. But although she was no longer the actual owner, she was still regarded as such. And if Mr D'Souza ever interfered, she dealt with him so severely that he hastily retreated into docility.

The adda continued to be known as Mai's Adda. And film folk, in their days of penury, continued to come there and drink on credit.

One night Mai died, quietly and peacefully. The news of her death spread through the industry like jungle fire. Cars started lining up from the crack of dawn. The Junior Artists Association, the Actors Guild, the Assistant Directors Association, etc., etc., all offered floral wreaths. David Abraham, Manmohan Krishna and Mahendranath lent their shoulders to carry her bier ... People said that such a grand funeral procession had never been seen in Danda. Photographs were published in *Blitz*!

SCENE: 75

Mai died. But Mai's Adda didn't. People had got used to Mai, so they began to call Mrs D'Souza 'Mai'. VD became Mrs D'Souza's, or rather Mai the Second's, favourite person. He had given her the impression that he wanted to marry her daughter, Rosy D'Souza. Which was why he was always given special treatment at the adda. D'Souza sahib didn't like VD much but, poor thing, what could he do?

VD was a born idler. He had worked in three films so far. And all three were speaking parts. In one of the films, he had played the villain's bodyguard. It was a role that should have had many lines. But the fucking writer was jealous of him. So, he made the character a mute. In the second film, he played a chowkidar who witnesses a murder. He screams, 'Murder,' and somebody shoots him. According to VD, the chowkidar was the real hero of the film because he had a two-year-old son who, when he grew up, vowed not to rest until he had found his father's killers. So, in a sense, the film was about the chowkidar, wasn't it? In the third film, he played compounder to the hero's doctor. Most of the doctor's time was taken up in wooing the heroine and singing songs with her, and it was left to the compounder to take care of the patients. He had quite a few lines of dialogue in this film. Someone would ask, 'Is doctor sahib in,' and he would say, 'No, he isn't.' (He said this on five occasions.) That's why VD thought of himself as a character actor. Mai the Second was very fond of watching movies. And she wanted Rosy to become a heroine. This was enough for VD. He became Rosy's PRO, and also began teaching her Hindi and Urdu. Mai stopped charging him for drinks.

'What is this vulgar, foolish thing you're doing?' Ali Amjad demanded of VD one night. It was VD's turn on the bed with the mosquito net. 'Why are you showing the poor thing these false dreams?'

'But why does she see them?' VD silenced everyone with this simple answer. 'My question is, why, in this country of the unemployed, in Bharat that is India, does any girl's mother have the right to name her daughter Rosy?'

VD was a strange fellow. He was always grave, as if the revolution would seek him out and land up at his very doorstep, as if in all of India no one else was waiting for a revolution except him.

Sometimes Alimullah would get angry with him, 'Come off it, yaar! Even if the revolution does come, one look at your seriousness will scare it away.'

That was why everyone was so surprised when VD started flirting with Rosy. VD and deception? Out of the question! But VD just kept saying that he liked her name. He would spend hours telling Rosy about the day's events. 'Today B.R. Chopra made a pukka commitment to give you a break in his next film. And Nasir Husain said, "Bring her over right now, I want to sign her for my next film." But he makes such escapist films. I won't let you work there...'

Ali Amjad and Harish could put up with all this. But Alimullah was an MA in political science. He used to call Gandhi an agent of the bourgeoisie, and Nehru a British spy. He would get irritated. He would say, 'VD, your Marxism is a fraud. Goddammit, Rosy isn't some kind of sex pill you can just pop...'

VD would smile and say, 'Rosy is a very talented girl. Talent should always be allowed a taste of the dew of asha, of hope...'

'So make her Asha Parekh's secretary, then. You're doing all this just for free booze, you fucker...'

VD and Alimullah didn't get along at all, not for a minute. But Alimullah was the only one who had a job. He would finance the other three at the end of the month. For each one of them, the end of the month came on different days. Harish got his salary on the fifteenth of every month. So, his month-end was the second or third of every month. Sometimes his month-end would stretch for several months because you couldn't be sure of your salary at small and medium-sized film companies. VD's month-end was more or less the whole year. For Ali Amjad, the month-end actually came at the end of every month. But it was only Alimullah who got a regular salary of 850 rupees. He also managed to earn an additional fifty or hundred. He was the one who largely bore the burden that was VD. They had studied together. They were both from Rasra, in Ballia district, and had come to Bombay together. They were extremely fond of each other, but also fought incessantly.

It was VD who had introduced Harish and Ali Amjad to Alimullah. One night, Ali Amjad and Harish were at Mai's Adda, writing out a proposal for their film. VD was sitting nearby, drinking. Nobody knows how, why and when he ended up sitting with them and becoming a 33 1/3 per cent partner in their project.

That night, both Ali Amjad and Harish were without a home. It was to avoid facing this brutal reality that they were sitting around arguing over the film proposal.

The difference between taking Rajendra Kumar or not taking him was seven and a half lakhs. Overflow separate. Ali Amjad was saying that they should take Rajendra Kumar. Harish was saying Rajendra Kumar was a fool. He didn't know how to act ... Slowly their voices grew louder. Harish Rai was the director. Ali Amjad the writer...

VD said, 'There's a new boy. Rajesh Khanna. You'll get him cheap ... Come, let's go home and talk at leisure.'

Cut.

D'Cruz Guest House. Room number five.

'This is Alimullah Khan,' said VD. 'He stays with me. And – Oh! I haven't even asked you your names. Anyway, what difference does that make? This one's a very famous director, and this one's a very well-known writer. They will stay with us now...'

Cut.

Ali Amjad took his leave from the memories of Mai's Adda, Mrs D'Souza and D'Cruz Guest House because the moon had left the clump of coconut trees and gone, god knows where. Outside, the night had fallen asleep. Inside, in the room, he was awake.

He picked the pen up again. He read what he had written.

SCENE: 75: DAY: POST OFFICE

The scene begins with the munshi sitting by the road, one leg folded under him, the other raised and bent at the knee. Across his knee lies a writing board upon which he is writing a letter…

He started writing.

Abulkhair's mother is sitting in front of him, grinding a rolled-up paan in a brass bowl, and dictating the letter.

ABULKHAIR'S MOTHER: What have you written, beta?

MUNSHI (*begins reading*): Salaam-alaikum to Abulkhair's abba, who should know that I am getting this letter written by the new Munshiji. The older one has gone back to his native place. So this letter might be short, but that doesn't mean it isn't important.

He looks up at Abulkhair's mother.

ABULKHAIR'S MOTHER: Yes, write. He should think of the letter as a telegram.

SCENE: 75

'Get out!' Bholanath Khatak's voice rang out.

Ali Amjad cursed the mothers and sisters of the wall in front of him even as, on the other side of that wall, Khatakji and Rama Chopra were creating their very own scene. All the other residents of the building had got used to Bholanath and Rama's fights. But Ali Amjad was new, and their fights bothered him.

Manchandani had warned him while handing over the keys to the flat, but he hadn't understood. Why, even D'Cruz Guest House was better than this! There you heard the noise of the street. The room had bedbugs. It had Mrs D'Cruz ... But one Bholanath Chopra more than made up for all of them.

Though his name was Bholanath Chopra, everyone in Sursingar Cooperative Housing Society Private Limited called him Bholanath Khatak or Khatakji because, in Hindi, 'khatak' meant 'irk' and he irked everyone.

What Bholanath Khatak really wanted, in his heart of hearts, was that no one else should live in Sursingar except for him. He thought of even his wife and children as his own begrudgingly. He could hardly stand the idea of anyone who was not his wife or child living in the building. But he was middle-class in his thinking. He knew there was no way he could stay alone there. The housing society had twenty-four flats in all, meant for twenty-four families, and twenty-four families did live there. And those twenty-four families had their own servants and maids and cooks.

Khatakji could have even tolerated the presence of so many people, but the problem was that all the servants only looked up to their own employers, whereas Khatakji wanted all of them to look up to him and acknowledge *him* as their boss. This was not acceptable to the servants of the building.

But doomsday truly arrived when Ali Amjad moved into the flat next to his. He had no children, but he had quite a few servants.

When Khatakji heard that Ali Amjad had shifted into the flat next to his, he muttered darkly to himself – because he was quite fond of muttering darkly to himself. The people of Sursingar had christened him Bhunbhun Chopra to begin with, because 'bhunbhun' in Hindi means 'muttering darkly'. Later, Mrs Gupta gave him the title of Khatakji and that name was unanimously adopted by everyone.

Rama Chopra, aka Mrs Khatak, was of the opinion that something had happened to her dear husband after coming to Sursingar. He hadn't been like this before.

Ramnath, a well-known film writer and resident of flat number twelve in Sursingar, did some digging around and discovered that:

Before coming to Sursingar, Khatakji used to live in a neighbourhood meant for Grade C clerks. He was a bill collector in an electronics company. His salary was 192 rupees, topped by allowances. Rama had announced to the neighbourhood at large that his salary was actually 1,092 rupees. This was in addition to allowances and 'extra' income earned on the side. They were newly married. Rama had new saris and new jewellery. They had a bit of money too. Things were good. Rama had very cleverly put up money at 50 per cent interest. The wives of clerks were always in need of money. That's why there was a great deal of respect for Rama in the neighbourhood. And Khatakji too was respected because clerks are used to bowing their heads subserviently. They keep shifting their soul around to make place for the files in their office, so much so that they don't even realize when it falls under a table. And the next day the sweeper throws it away with yesterday's trash. But these men without a soul are forever ready to scrutinize other people's souls. It was the same situation in his neighbourhood. Everyone respected him, everyone would scrutinize him. And this tin god of the neighbourhood, oblivious to everything, would fly the flag of his five-foot-eleven-inch body from the rooftop.

And then one day, a clerk from that neighbourhood found himself in the vicinity of Khatakji's office around lunchtime. Shri Babulal Srivastava did receive a lunch allowance from his office but, he thought, why shouldn't he save it? And he thought this because the office of his neighbour who earned 1,092 rupees was close by. So, he set off for Bholanath's office. But when he imperiously asked the peon for Deputy Sales Supervisor Mr Bholanath Chopra, the peon brusquely brushed his query aside, as if he were brushing aside a fly: there was no deputy sales supervisor by that name. Yes, there was an assistant bill collector of the same name. Shri Babulal Srivastava, the clerk, thought the peon was joking. He was upset that a mere peon had the audacity to joke with a Grade C clerk. The peon also got riled. There was a heated exchange. Thankfully, Khatakji arrived at the scene exactly at that moment, or things could have got out of hand. The instant Khatakji saw Shri Babulal, he broke into a sweat. He didn't give the peon a chance to say another word, just hurriedly scolded him and ushered Srivastavaji away.

SCENE: 75

There was a cheap teashop nearby, as well as a Kwality. Normally he went to the cheap teashop and ate usal-pav, but since Srivastavaji was with him, he had to go to Kwality. After all, how could a man who earned 1,092 rupees (allowances and commissions extra) eat usal-pav?

In his entire working life of ten years, Khatakji had been to Kwality only once, that too to drink a cup of tea. Men who earned 192 rupees didn't eat at restaurants like Kwality, they just read the menu board and moved on.

'What would you like to eat?' asked Khatakji. He felt like he was risking his life with that question.

'Let's have tandoori chicken,' Srivastavaji said. He knew nothing of restaurants like this, except that they would serve tandoori chicken. Then he picked up the menu card. Khatakji too had a menu card in his hand. Srivastavaji was giving the order and, as he spoke, Khatakji was doing some quick mental arithmetic.

Two tandoori chickens – 18 rupees.

'No, Srivastavaji. Today is Tuesday. I don't eat meat on Tuesdays.'

'Come on. What age are you living in...' Srivastava sahib began again:

Two shahi kormas –14 rupees.

Two butter chickens – 22 rupees.

Bholanath Khatak was drowning in the deep well of Srivastavaji's voice and his heart was wandering, lost, in the desert of his pocket ... His appetite vanished just listening to the order.

The bill, when it came, was for 87.16 rupees. Luckily Khatakji had just returned from a bill-collecting tour, so he had the money. He drew out a wad of hundred-rupee notes from his pocket. Then he selected the oldest note from the wad and paid the bill.

Shri Babulal, the clerk, had never seen so many hundred-rupee notes in one place in his entire life. And when Khatakji tipped the waiter five rupees and eighty-four paise, he almost fainted.

Ninety-three rupees had been spent on the meal, but it created an impression in the neighbourhood. Rama got the news late because she had gone for a matinee show with Mrs Sarla Midha. It had been decided that Khatakji would meet them outside Neptune Talkies, after which they would repair to Midha sahib's home for dinner.

Rama ensured that she made such plans with Sarla at least two or three times a week. There were several advantages to this. The cinema was free. The evening dinner was free. The whisky was free. And what kind of whisky? Real Scotch. Dimple, Johnnie Walker, and sometimes even Chivas Regal.

Khatakji knew the names of good whiskies by heart. He bought empty bottles from Chor Bazaar, filled them with tea and decorated his bar with them. In his own home, he drank only Indian whisky, and that too only once every couple of months. But after Rama became friends with Sarla, Khatakji only had to remind her that she hadn't seen a film for about two days and Rama would rush off to the neighbourhood public phone booth and call Sarla, 'Listen, there's a really good film running in Bandra Talkies.'

And Sarla would promptly get ready to go to the cinema.

The thing was that poor Sarla had problems of her own. Midha sahib found other men's wives beautiful. Which was why he never had any time for her. In a way, this was fine with Sarla – because she had no interest in men either. She liked other men's wives too. This was a pleasure to which she had been introduced by a Sophia College teacher, Miss D'Cruz.

Miss D'Cruz used to teach literature. If you didn't do your class work, she would pinch your cheeks in an odd way. If she was happy, she would give you a clinging hug that was also a bit odd. In private, the senior girls referred to her as 'Mr D'Cruz'. At first Mrs Midha (who, in those days, was just simple, innocent Sarla) didn't understand why the senior girls called her that. When she mustered the courage to ask, she got a strange laugh in response ... Then she found that the shrivelled and sour Miss Ruqaiya Dilgir seemed to have become unnecessarily jealous of her. Even if she did her work properly, Miss Dilgir would find some excuse to scold her. She would give her more homework than anyone else. She would object to her clothes.

Sarla couldn't understand Ruqaiya's anger, and she would complain tearfully to Miss D'Cruz who would smile, envelop Sarla in her arms, and kiss her on the lips. Or she would gently bite Sarla's lips, or stick her tongue into her mouth, and Sarla's young, inexperienced body would tremble with a strange kind of excitement ... And Miss Dilgir would sulk even more.

Then one day, in the staff room, in front of all the other teachers, Miss D'Cruz took Miss Dilgir severely to task for unduly persecuting Sarla. Miss Dilgir began to cry. Miss D'Cruz turned away and began to laugh and chat with another teacher.

SCENE: 75

Before Sarla came along, Miss D'Cruz and Miss Dilgir were very close. And Miss Dilgir didn't look the wreck she did now. She looked like a young girl. A dusky, big-eyed, slender young girl. Then Sarla arrived, and Miss Dilgir found herself all alone. The spark in her eyes died, it was as if a lightbulb in her eyes had fused.

One day when Sarla came back from the reading room, she found – to her surprise – Miss Dilgir fast asleep on her bed. There was a letter on the table. Sarla began reading. It was addressed to her:

'Sarla, it wasn't right of you to steal Liz from me. You are the one who stole my life, so why should I go anywhere else to die? Now, when Liz will take you in her arms or kiss your mouth or put her hand inside your blouse or … The very thought suffocates me. May god destroy you, Sarla … When you respond to Liz's love-making with that unripe, childish body of yours, you will see me, in your bed, lying between Liz and you, dead…'

Sarla couldn't read any more. Leaving Dilgir's corpse on her bed, she ran out and kept running until she found herself outside Miss D'Cruz's room – Mr D'Cruz for senior girls, and Liz for Miss Dilgir.

Liz was the warden of New Block. Between New Block and Old Block was an old tamarind tree, and stories about this tree ran rife through the hostel. It was supposed to house a djinn or a ghost whose job it was to trouble the girls. But that night, Sarla didn't even notice the tree, though during the day she always took pains to keep her distance from it.

She began beating on the door. Liz opened it. She saw Sarla's state and was overcome with fear. Without a word, Sarla handed her Dilgir's letter ... And that night, Sarla understood why the senior girls called Liz 'Mr D'Cruz'.

For many weeks, Sophia College was shrouded in silence. Liz had torn up Dilgir's letter that very night. Everyone knew why Dilgir had committed suicide, and everyone knew why she had done so in Sarla's room, but no one said a word. What could anyone have said anyway? After a while, they forgot about Miss Dilgir, and the senior girls began referring to Sarla as 'Mrs D'Cruz'.

So, how could she have been interested in Mr Midha! She had come to her husband's home with a sixteen-year-old maidservant who looked after her, and took care of all her needs. Midha couldn't even say anything, because it was only by making Sarla Mrs Midha that he'd got the money to start his business. So, when he found out that he hadn't really got a wife, he began taking an interest in other men's wives. He did make sure, though, to stay away from those wives on whom Sarla herself had an eye.

Midha liked bill collector Bholanath's wife, Rama. He felt as if she was made of M-foam. Her skin was pale like a champa flower. Her eyes looked as if they understood the language of eyes. He decided to befriend Bholanath.

One day, Midha came to the Grade C Officers Housing Cooperative Society in his Ford convertible, looking for Bholanath's flat. Residents of the society had seen such a car only on the road, or in Hindi and English movies. But this car was parked bang in the middle of their neighbourhood. Everyone was awed into silence. And when they got to know that the man in the car had come to visit Bholanath, their respect for him rose even further. Soon, Midha became a regular visitor. At first he would come only when Bholanath was at home, then he used the I-was-just-passing-by-thought-I'd-drop-in excuse a couple of times. Then he completely stopped coming when Khatakji was home.

Around this time, Sarla and Rama finally met each other. Rama was in Mehrabad Bazaar looking at

American georgette saris. She couldn't afford to buy any, so she just looked at them, delighting in imagining herself wearing French chiffon, georgette, Kanjeevaram, Mysore silk and Banarasi saris. She had a system. She never went to the same shop more than once a month ... After two months, who would remember that a certain Rama Chopra had come and looked at some hundred-odd saris without buying a single one? Sensibly, Rama only spent time in shops that were already crowded. While looking at the saris, she would offer advice to the woman sitting next to her – this silk is not so fine, the motifs on this one are a bit faulty, yes that one is nice ... and it's forty rupees cheaper in that other shop. She knew the prices of saris in every shop, which ones had new stock and which ones didn't ... The shopkeeper would curse inwardly when he heard her. But because he thought that Rama was with the woman buying saris, he wouldn't say anything, and she would also get a glass of cold Coke along with that other woman. She would drink the Coke and leave the shop when the other woman left. And because the woman had saved some thirty or forty rupees on account of Rama, she would be forced to ask her, 'Where do you stay?' Rama was always apprehensive about this query. She didn't want to reveal that she lived in a Grade C Officers Housing Cooperative Society. So she would say, 'What can I say, behenji, it's so difficult to find a place to stay in Bombay. We've booked three flats. One on Peddar Road, one on Cuffe Parade, and one in Juhu. But they're not ready yet. We're staying with a relative in Bandra East. It's such a bother…' In the course of the conversation, she would extract the woman's name and address, and write down her phone number. And if it turned out that she was well-to-do, Rama would ring her up once or twice. Then she would start visiting her off and on, and thus, lunch and evening tea would be taken care of … But she had never met Sarla because Midha sahib never wanted that to happen. Midha sahib liked Rama. But just as he was a devotee of fine liquor, he was also a devotee of the fine art of debauchery. He didn't favour the kind of alcohol that went straight to your head after the first sip, neither was he turned on by women who responded to the first smile with a 'where's the bedroom?' More than the destination, it was the journey that he enjoyed. And currently, he was still journeying towards Rama. He was still mixing butter into the sarson ka saag. That's why he wanted to slip away with Sarla when he spotted Rama in a shop – also because Sarla was in a bad mood that day.

Her maidservant had run away with a man, and Sarla was without a partner. And in such circumstances, he was even more determined that the two women should not meet. But Rama spotted him. Smiling, she all but jumped up and made her way towards him. She had been looking for a way to escape from the salesman who had succeeded in making her zero in on one particular sari. She couldn't think of any excuse to give him. She was thinking of opening her purse and exclaiming, 'Arre! I forgot to bring money! Will a cheque do?' She knew a cheque would never do. She had often pulled out a cheque book and seen this for herself. While writing the cheque, she would say, 'Okay, let me do something. I'll come back in half an hour and take the sari. Otherwise, I know your heart will be racing, wondering whether the cheque will be cashed or not…' And the relieved shopkeeper would say, 'Arre, behenji, what are you saying? This is your shop. Take whatever you want. The money isn't going to run away anywhere…' At the same time, he would stop wrapping the sari and toss it aside. 'As you wish, then. You can come after half an hour.' And there the matter would end. But this particular shopkeeper had not only agreed to accept a cheque, he was insisting he wouldn't let Rama leave without the sari. So Rama had been forced to write a cheque. Which wasn't a problem, except she had only twenty-seven rupees and twenty-four paise in the bank and the sari cost 118 rupees. That's why Rama swooped down on Midha like a kite the moment she saw him. The shopkeeper said to his salesman, 'That bitch, there's no way she'll come back to buy the sari now.'

And that was how Sarla and Rama met in Mehrabad, and Sarla took an immediate liking to Rama. Seeing Sarla smile, it was as if a blanket of frost smothered Midha's ardour. He understood that nothing would come of his pursuit of Rama now. And so, Sarla and Rama became friends. Sarla's car began frequenting the neighbourhood. Sarla began taking Rama to watch films, presenting saris to her ... But, every now and then, they would taunt each other too. Rama because she wanted to show everyone that she herself spent money on someone like Sarla who came to visit her in a big car, and Sarla so that no one would suspect what she was actually thinking about Rama. The story about the maidservant had spread, and all the mothers in the building had begun hiding their daughters from her. And Sarla didn't want Rama to find out so soon.

Then one day, it so happened that Sarla had gone for a puja. Rama hadn't been able to accompany her because she wasn't feeling well. Taking advantage of the situation, Midha landed up at Rama's house on the pretext that Sarla was enquiring about her health. Rama's head was hurting. He insisted on massaging it ... The blood in his body hadn't starting racing, but yes, his hands did occasionally slide from Rama's head to her neck. She had a beautiful neck ... And then Bholanath arrived. Midha panicked. Bholanath and Rama fought the whole day. The next day was Rakshabandhan. Midha got Rama to tie a rakhi on him.

The truth was that poor Rama was actually quite blameless. In fact, Rama thought there wasn't a handsomer man in the world than Bholanath. And Bholanath whole-heartedly agreed with Rama. He thought pretty much the same of Rama too. That's why, the minute Bholanath became suspicious of any man, he would immediately get Rama to tie a rakhi on him. Now let's see that fucker try to romance his 'sister'! After a while, everyone caught on to what it meant when Rama tied a rakhi on someone.

When Midha got a rakhi tied by Rama, Sarla breathed a sigh of relief. She had had a slight suspicion that perhaps Rama was interested in him. That's why she'd proceeded with caution – so that if Rama was not interested, she could quickly shift her position. She'd contented herself with styling Rama's hair for hours. Giving her facials. Removing blackheads. Saying, 'How have you tied your sari? Punjabis will never learn how to tie one!' Rama would laugh. Sarla would laugh with her. Rama would take off her sari. Sarla would say, 'My, my, Rama, look at your waist...' Rama would be delighted. She liked her waist very much. Laughing, Sarla would place a hand there and say, 'It must be a problem for him, trying to find your waist!' And she would start tickling Rama, who would collapse on the bed, doubled up with laughter, and in helping her to straighten up, Sarla would keep sliding her hands all over her body...

The first advantage Rama took of Sarla's friendship was learning how to tie a sari properly. She learnt the importance of matching her chappals with her sari's border. She also discovered which shade of lipstick matched which shade of sari ... And the second advantage she took was this – because of Midha's recommendation, Bholanath Khatak was appointed as an assistant sales supervisor in a company that manufactured blades. He started earning more. Rama also took advantage of Sarla's affections by borrowing 10,000 rupees from her and putting it up on interest. That's how she was able to book a flat in Sursingar Cooperative Housing Society Private Limited.

Manchandani had the contract for the building's plumbing. Rama wanted to see her flat being made in front of her eyes. So, both of them would be in Sursingar all day. Manchandani was a jovial guy. Rama was an affable woman. They became friends. Rama hoped that, because they were friends, Manchandani would use the same materials for her flat as he was using for his own. And why would Manchandani object, when Rama's smile glimmered with the fragrant gold of wheat fields? A smile like an open book. And what was the harm if he could spend a few moments with this smiling Rama? Until then, Manchandani hadn't found out that Rama was not 'that' kind of girl ... That she had drawn a Lakshman-rekha around herself ... That while she certainly wanted the golden deer, she would not step beyond the boundaries she had set for herself to get it. She would chat and laugh with Manchandani, give him tea, but in the evening she would go home with Bholanath Khatak ... There were no leaks in the plumbing of her soul.

But Bholanath was Bholanath. After a few days, a suspicion began burrowing under his skin like an insect. God knows what was happening in that flat! But nobody ever had a cure for suspicion, not even Hakim Luqman, so how was poor Rama supposed to?

As Khatakji's suspicions deepened, they stuck to the envelope of his personality like a postage stamp ... And Rama soon figured out that something was wrong. So, on Rakshabandhan, she tied a rakhi on Manchandani and ended the matter once and for all. But she was hurt, even though she was used to Khatakji's suspicious nature. Because of it, she had tied rakhis on three men. Every night, even after eating to his heart's content, he would continue to berate her ... So much so that by the time it was morning, she would be diminished to one-third or one-fourth of herself. And then, only after a day of strenuous striving, would she somehow make herself whole again.

Khatakji – the very thought of spending an entire lifetime with a man like that was a brave one. How was poor Rama expected to remember what she said to the fruit-seller while smiling ... Why she appeared in front of the postman in just her petticoat and blouse ... Inwardly, she would fret at this humiliation – was she only fit for fruit-sellers, postmen and neighbourhood servants? She would start crying. When she cried, Khatakji's temper would rise. And as it rose, Rama would start fretting even more. And a mahabharat would ensue. And when that happened, everyone in the neighbourhood would sprout thousands of ears. So even someone who earned 1,092 rupees fought with his wife! This was proof positive that it was wives who created trouble...

During these fights, at first Rama would curse softly and Khatakji would roar in Punjabi, Hindi and English. But when, fed up, she too would start cursing loudly, Khatakji's voice would begin to grow softer and softer. He would suddenly be worried about his neighbours' ears.

The next day, he would examine his neighbours' faces to figure out if they had heard him and Rama fighting, and if so, what exactly they had heard. But the Grade C officers were skilled in the art of telling barefaced lies. Khatakji would be convinced that nobody knew of his fight with Rama, and he'd be ready, once again, to work himself up over some new suspicion and blow it out of proportion.

But when Shri Babulal Srivastava, the clerk, hit him where it hurt by eating lunch at Kwality, Khatakji developed a hatred for all his neighbours, who salaamed him every morning and evening, whose children ran errands for his household, whose wives sucked up to Rama, and without whose help it would have been impossible for him to live in that neighbourhood.

Still, buying lunch for 87 rupees and 16 paise was another matter altogether. Spending one rupee more than half his salary on just one lunch!

He'd smiled in front of Shri Babulal Srivastava the clerk, and said, 'Arre, Babulalji, what do these poor waiters earn. They survive on tips. And, sahib, it's simple, if you tip well, you get good service…' With these words, Khatakji got up. Babulalji got up too, thinking that if a waiter served food to twenty people and if he got three, if not five, rupees on average per meal, then in a month he would make 20 multiplied by 3, that is 60, multiplied by 30, which meant about 1,800 rupees in just tips … Which meant that a waiter at Kwality earned more than Bholanath!

And Khatakji, on his part, was being eaten up by the thought of where and how he would get 93 rupees.

That evening, Bholanath was found unconscious in a local train compartment. For about half an hour he couldn't remember who or where he was. His watch and all the money from his pocket was missing. The fake diamond ring he wore on his third finger was gone too. The police came. The doctor came. About two hours passed. Slowly he became aware of his surroundings and remembered who he was, and then he remembered that he had been carrying 18,500 rupees from his company in his pocket. Statements were recorded. A report was prepared. All Bholanath could remember was that he had run out of cigarettes. A fellow passenger had offered him one from his packet. First, he'd taken one for himself, then extended the pack to him. He'd been desperate for a smoke. So he took one. He smoked it. He chatted with the fellow passenger ... He had no recollection of what happened after that. The police asked him to describe this fellow passenger. He said he was tall. Stout. A nose like a parrot's beak. A big moustache ... Bholanath stopped. The police thought he was trying to remember. The truth was he had stopped because he'd realized he was describing Midha ... But now that he had started, he had to go on. So, he described Midha in full detail. At one point, he felt like giving the police Midha's name and address as well. But he realized that the police would never believe that a wealthy wife's husband could have drugged an assistant bill collector. So, he didn't go beyond the description.

There was a journalist at the scene. He took a photo of Khatakji, who was thrilled because, at least in this way, he would get his picture in the papers. Then the people of his neighbourhood would realize what an honour it was for them to live with Bholanath. While talking to the journalist, he furtively looked at his watch only to find a bare wrist, and then he smiled inwardly, because his watch and the 18,500 rupees were safe in a second-hand suitcase in a Bombay Central cloakroom.

While all of this was going on, someone from his office also landed up. The police registered a case. Khatakji was given permission to leave. He took an advance of ten rupees from the man from his office so that he could go home. It was 7 p.m. by the journalist's watch. This meant that Rama would have gone with Sarla to her house, learning how to tie a sari or figuring out lipstick shades in her bedroom, while Midha would be downing Scotch.

The thought of Scotch made Bholanath very thirsty.

Lisa opened the door.

Lisa was Sarla's new maid. She was Catholic. When she went for confession, she would leave out anything to do with Sarla. But she would giggle and tell her boyfriend all about her. And then both of them would laugh. Midha too tried to flirt lightly with her.

Khatakji liked Lisa as well. Because of her, he had started seeing the Midhas more frequently. On her birthday, he had given Lisa a rosebud and, in front of Rama, Sarla and Midha, told her laughingly, in English, that he had fallen in love with her. Everyone guffawed at this, including Lisa who then stuck her tongue out at him. Since then, the thought of that tongue had been crawling all over Khatakji's body like an earthworm. Many a time, he had slept with Rama, making believe that she was Lisa. Once he had even called her Lisa. Luckily for Khatakji, Rama had been busy buttoning her blouse, so she didn't notice Khatakji's faux pas...

Lisa smiled when she saw him. He smiled back at her.

And that was where this love story had been stalled for the past year.

Inside, Midha sahib was drinking Scotch.

The sound of Rama and Sarla's laughter came from the bedroom.

Midha smiled when he saw Khatakji, though he felt no pleasure at seeing him. If he couldn't romance Rama, what was the point of looking happy when he saw her husband? Nevertheless, fearful of Sarla, he had to smile. So Midha did his duty and smiled.

'Ki haal...' Khatakji began in Punjabi. He always spoke to Midha in Punjabi because he knew Midha didn't like it. In this way, he also punished Midha for attempting to seduce Rama.

Midha was not a Punjabi, though his parents certainly were. He was born in a refugee camp in Delhi. His father began practising law in Lucknow, but the practice never took off. Midha grew up in Lucknow. And he began speaking the scrubbed and smoothly ironed-out khari boli of that city. He began humming couplets from 'Zehr-e-Ishq' and 'Gulzar-e-Naseem'.[1] He would argue about Aatish's poetry and go into a trance about Anis's marsiyas. He'd studied Urdu till his BA, and then married Sarla who considered Hindi and Urdu rude, rustic languages and spoke English at home. Midha liked English too. But because of Sarla's obstinacy, he began detesting English. That left Punjabi. By hating Punjabi, he was punishing his father who had fixed his marriage with Sarla ... One day, in an alcohol-induced

[1] Two famous masnavis in Urdu, one by Nawab Mirza 'Shauq' and the other by Dayashankar 'Naseem'.

state, he had poured his heart out to Khatakji. This was before Khatakji had seen him massaging Rama's head. And now, Bholanath was taking advantage of that.

Bholanath sat down, made himself comfortable, and began pouring himself a drink. For Midha, it was as if Bholanath was making a drink with his blood. But he kept smiling, because he had learnt to smile. The sound of Rama and Sarla's laughter kept wafting out of the bedroom…

'Just try it, darling.' That was Sarla's voice.

'I am worried about him.' Rama's voice.

Then all of a sudden, Sarla's laughter became vulgar, indecent, dirty. But Bholanath didn't have time to reflect on the nature of that laughter, because at that moment Lisa came in with ice and bent in order to put it on the table. She was wearing a low-cut dress and, as she bent, Bholanath caught a glimpse of her brassiere-covered breasts. Lisa understood what was going on. She stayed bent for a moment longer. And in that moment, all the blood in Bholanath and Midha's bodies rushed to their faces, their heartbeats started thudding in their temples, their throats went dry, and Lisa burst out laughing. Still laughing, she first looked at Midha, then at Bholanath. They were both peering down her blouse.

She straightened up and said, 'You naughty boys!' And she continued to laugh as she turned and went to the kitchen, their eyes following her. She knew they were watching, so she swayed her hips a little more sexily.

In the kitchen, Lisa told her boyfriend about the two men. Both of them laughed, and the sound of Lisa and Peter's laughter merged with Rama and Sarla's in the sitting room.

Peter's real name was Ramnath. He was from Kanpur. Many years ago, he had come to Bombay to become another Rajesh Khanna and romance Mumtaz. After arriving in the city, he'd parked himself in front of Rajesh Khanna's Carter Road house for some ten to twelve days. He didn't budge. He'd watch Rajesh Khanna go in and out. Then he got bored of hanging around the house and began doing the rounds of studios instead, where there were many young men like him. Since he had run away from home with a fair bit of money, he didn't have to deal with hunger. All day, he would look at film stars to his heart's content, and then find some place or the other to sleep at night. He wasn't harassed by any filmy-type constable or goon, and lost any fear he may have had of Bombay. He had studied up to middle school, and so in his spare time he began writing stories for films. One day, he was sitting in an Irani teahouse, treating some of his Bombay friends to usal-pav and narrating the story of a film he'd written which would be just right for Rajesh Khanna and Mumtaz. He didn't know that Shri Phanda Patialvi was sitting at the table behind him, writing a scene for one of his films. The scene went something like this: The hero is sitting in an Irani teahouse having breakfast while waiting for the crime boss. The hero is actually a CID inspector on a mission to find out about the boss, and that's why he joins his gang and does some smuggling, while romancing the heroine because she's the boss's daughter ... The hero's love life is also part of his duty ... All this was fine. But Shri Phanda Patialvi hadn't been to an Irani teahouse in about seven years. Before that, he hadn't been able to afford a cup of tea in an Irani teahouse. If he managed to badger a friend into taking him to one, he would have a tikona biscuit and a cup of tea. Then, one of his films became a hit and he bought a car. And now that he'd written seven or eight hit films, Irani teahouses were no longer good enough for Shri Phanda. Producers and stars chased after him. He would go for dinner to Rajesh Khanna's house. Dilip Kumar would show up at his child's birthday, carrying as a gift an expensive toy that had probably been smuggled into the city. If Sunil Dutt saw him from afar, he would wave. Dev Anand gave statements saying that there wasn't a better writer in Bombay than Shri Phanda Patialvi. Move over, Bhagwati babu, Yashpal, Amritlal Nagar, Manto, Krishan Chander, Ismat Chughtai, Rajinder Singh Bedi ... There was only one name worth mentioning in contemporary Hindi literature – Shri Phanda Patialvi. Shri Phanda was a revolutionary writer. He was the first one to introduce the lives and politics of the middle-class to Hindi films. *Mazdoor ka Beta, Kaatil Kaun, Chalees Alibaba Ek Chor, Kasam* ... After writing more than half a dozen revolutionary films, it struck Shri Phanda that he should now write something offbeat. He decided to direct it himself. And that was the story in which the wretched hero lands up in an Irani teahouse. Shri Phanda tried hard to remember what an Irani teahouse was like, but when he couldn't, he had to perforce visit one. His PRO sent a photographer too. He thought the pictures would help embellish Shri Phanda's image. And so there he was writing the scene, the photographer was taking pictures, Ramnath's voice was filtering through the din of the teahouse as if through a sieve, and Phanda Patialvi lost no time in deciding that Ramnath was narrating an original, solid, 'golden jubilee' subject. Phandaji put his pen down. The photographer kept taking pictures. Phandaji kept listening to Ramnath's story…

By the time he got up to leave the teahouse, Ramnath had a job as Phandaji's servant.

Ramnath was familiar with Phandaji's name because he had come to Bombay to become another Rajesh Khanna, and Rajesh Khanna had acted in several of Phandaji's hit films. That's why he accepted the job instantly. He was sure that Rajesh Khanna would be a regular visitor to Phandaji's house.

But Phandaji's intentions were quite different. He wanted no one in the film-making fraternity to get wind of Ramnath's genius. He took Ramnath in his Italian Fiat to his flat on the twenty-second floor of the building, Sea Breeze. The Arabian Sea in front. The city of Bombay at the back. Ramnath loved the flat, and decided that when he became a star he would buy one in the same building.

Because he had studied up to middle school, Ramnath was not skilled at any kind of work. Being the only son among three daughters, he had been spoilt silly at home. He was not expected to do anything. His father, Babu Chandrika Prasad, was a clerk in the Kanpur Municipal Corporation. He used to handle toll taxes and so, with god's blessings, the extra income was quite substantial. They had a pukka two-storey house in Chamanganj – Ramnath Bhawan. Ramnath knew that this house was his. So what was the need to work? When Phandaji's wife found out that he couldn't do anything, she was annoyed, more so because he was going to be paid fifty rupees a month. And they had a fifteen-year-old daughter at home ... But Phandaji paid no attention to his wife, and Ramnath had the first affair of his life with Phandaji's daughter, Pushplata. However, it would be wrong to say that Ramnath romanced Pushplata, because she wasn't the sort that anybody would want to romance. She paid him to romance her. Ramnath began getting fifty rupees a month from Pushplata as well. And hundred rupees a month was definitely better than fifty.

Poor Pushplata had her own problems. All her friends had a crush on someone or the other. They would go and watch films with their boyfriends. They would have necking sessions with them on the Bandstand rocks. A couple of them even went beyond necking. Some of them smoked hash. A few had started tripping on LSD. They would talk to each other in National College, and poor Pushplata would feel left out because she had no stories or experiences worth sharing.

Pushplata was not a good-looking girl, and in Phandaji's stories the heroine was never bad-looking, so she couldn't even imagine herself as a heroine ... Her life was slipping by, empty and lonely. Without any direction. Without any meaning. Phandaji had no time to think about her problems, and her mother was so tied up in gossiping with neighbours, buying saris, and getting jewellery made that she sometimes quite forgot that she was the mother of a young girl.

Radhika, Pushplata's mother, had an attractive face and body. She looked like her daughter's older sister. If she did her make-up a little carefully, she looked like her younger sister. That's why, in her heart of hearts, she was happy about Pushplata's lack of looks, because if she'd had a beautiful young daughter who called her 'mummy', she would've found it hard to hide her age. As things were, whether a producer came home, or a hero, or an upcoming star, they would talk only to her, laugh only with her, and for that moment, she would become a Mumtaz or a Sharmila Tagore or a Hema Malini, and her lonely, disappointed life would, for a moment, recede into the distance – the songs of *Heer* would begin to seem old-fashioned, and she would get up, go to the record player and put on some Western music. She didn't like it, nor did she understand it, but fashion was fashion after all. She would criticize Naushad, Jaidev, Khayyam and Sajjad, and lavish praise on RD (Burman), LP (Laxmikant-Pyarelal) and Kalyanji-Anandji. She would give everybody the impression that she tied rakhis on Rajesh Khanna and was great friends with LP.

In other words, Radhika had no time to think about Pushplata and, on her part, Pushplata found herself quite alone in the loud, raucous sound of her mother's brazen laughter. That's why, when Phandaji brought Ramnath to the house, Pushplata thrilled to an unknown pleasure. At first, Pushplata couldn't understand the reason behind this happiness, but the fact that she felt happy was enough for her.

Ramnath didn't spare her a glance, spending time in the bathroom, lost in thoughts of Mumtaz instead. The rest of his time was spent with Phandaji, who would inevitably steer the subject back to stories, and Ramnath would begin narrating his 'original' plots, and Phandaji would then toss in Chase, Carter Brown, Gardner, Christie, and start stirring.

Ramnath worked in Phandaji's home for one and a half years. During this time, Phandaji sold seven 'original' stories and put all other film writers out of business. He was the subject of discussion at every film party, and people were heard saying that Phandaji Patialvi had begun charging four and a half lakhs. Ramnath didn't even realize that he had become a famous film writer in Phandaji's name because he was now spending a lot of time in Pushplata's room.

Phandaji was never around, day or night. Radhika also spent most of her time with her neighbours. There was no one in the flat except for Ramnath. When Pushplata returned from college, the thought that she would be alone in the flat with him was enough to make her tingle. She would keep calling him to her room on some pretext or the other. He would go. Soon, he understood what Pushplata wanted. But he wasn't any old discarded thing that could be picked up by anyone. And even to pick up something that had been discarded, you had to bend. That's why he decided that to get him, Pushplata would have to bend ... Things continued like this for a few days. Pushplata would smile coyly whenever she saw him. She would allow her hand to touch his while taking a glass of water ... Then one day, the hook on her blouse got stuck and she had to call Ramnath. He came.

SCENE: 75

'What is it, bibiji?'

Both of Pushplata's hands were struggling with the hook at the back of her blouse.

'This hook has got stuck,' she steeled herself to say. Her throat was dry. Her breath was shallow, her temples throbbed and seemed ready to burst with the pressure of her racing blood, and she was filled with a strange, sweet fear. As she heard Ramnath's footsteps approach, that sweet fear swelled...

'What are you doing, someone will see us!'

'Don't pretend,' he said heartlessly. 'There's no one else here but me.' Ramnath took her blouse off.

He had no experience in these matters. He had just heard a few casual comments, and he'd heard abuses on the streets of Kanpur ... He decided he would put those obscenities to the test.

So he tried them out, and found them to be truthful and pleasurable ... And in the course of that undisturbed afternoon, Ramnath's income went up by fifty rupees.

Ramnath wasn't unhappy with this life. He would sometimes imagine Pushplata as Mumtaz, sometimes as Sharmila Tagore or Waheeda Rehman ... Once or twice she was even Helen, Hema Malini and Bindu.

Pushplata was playing the same game. She too would close her eyes and Ramnath's hands would sometimes become Dharmendra's and sometimes Rajesh Khanna's...

Meaning, both were happy. Perhaps the two of them would have continued to be happy in this fashion for many days, but one night Radhika returned from a party, her body taut like a string. Dharmendra had put his hand on her shoulder, gazed into her eyes and said, 'Bhabhiji, you are quite something...' And this resounded in her head all the way home. In her heart of hearts, she had already asked Dharmendra, 'What am I?' a thousand times, and Dharmendra had laughed and inched close. So close that he was almost on top of her and her breath stopped. Her fingers dug deep into the velvet of the car seat ... She didn't even realize when the car stopped and her elderly driver got out and opened the door for her ... At that moment, even old Ali Muhammad seemed devastatingly young to Radhika, and she smiled at him.

'Shall I park the car for the night?' Ali Muhammad asked.

She heard her voice saying, 'Yes.'

In the privacy of the lift, Dharmendra once again crushed her in his arms. And she felt as if she wasn't in a lift but floating on a cloud of fat, fluffy cushions, and the cloud, like Dharmendra's breath, was rising. The lift stopped as she held her breath and kept saying to Dharmendra, 'What are you doing ji…'

The building's watchman was standing outside the lift, waiting for Radhika to come out. But when she kept standing and smiling, he got worried and opened the door. At the sound of the door opening, Radhika came to with a start and got out of the lift. The watchman stared after her, bewildered…

Radhika rang the bell. Once. She waited for a moment. The door didn't open. She rang the bell, longer this time. The door still didn't open. Irritated, she pressed down on the buzzer until Ramnath finally opened the door. The buttons of his shirt were undone, and Radhika could glimpse the golden hair peeping out. She was still drunk on Dharmendra and forgot to scold him. She smiled and said:

'Were you asleep?'

Ramnath shook his head.

She went inside.

'Idiot!' she said, bringing her face close to his, and Ramnath's head began ringing with the obscenities he'd heard on the streets of Kanpur. 'Does anyone sleep so early?' she asked. She let her pallu slide down, then flung it over her shoulder in such a manner that Ramnath almost got trapped in its folds, and started laughing.

'Get me a glass of water before you go to sleep,' she said as she went into her room. Ramnath went to the kitchen. Pushplata was waiting for him in her bed, and Phandaji was sitting in some hero's house, looking at a starlet who kept laughing at the hero's words and kept bending to pick something up, her blouse dipping and the hero peeping, while Phandaji narrated the story...

'Come in,' Radhika said when there was a knock on the door. She was lying in bed, wearing a transparent nightie. Actually, Hema Malini's dressmaker had made this nightie for the star. She was supposed to wear it in a film. But the shooting got postponed and when, three months later, the time came to wear the nightie, it was discovered that it had become too small. Radhika knew the dressmaker and so she bought it. And one night she wore the nightie, just like that, and lay down on her bed ... for Phandaji. But Phandaji didn't even notice. He came out of the bathroom in his underpants and Radhika suddenly began to feel very naked. She pursed her lips at the memory. Ramnath was standing in front of her, holding a glass of cold water. Radhika stretched, her nightie climbed up, and her bare calves came into view. Radhika liked her legs, particularly her calves. She caught Ramnath staring at them.

'My legs are really hurting today. Massage them a bit,' she said and shifted on the bed to make some space for Ramnath, whose ears once again began ringing with those Kanpuri obscenities...

Pushplata waited, wide awake. She fretted. When she couldn't bear it any more, she went out of her room. She peered into the kitchen. Ramnath's bed was empty. The bathroom door was ajar. Ramnath wasn't in the sitting room either. Her mother's bedroom door was shut. She tiptoed towards it. She peeped in through the keyhole. She couldn't see the bed but she heard the sound of her mother laughing. She recognized that laughter. It was like her own ... The one which bubbled over when Ramnath unbuttoned her blouse.

She stood stunned, because now Ramnath was her lover as well as her stepfather. Radhika was her mother as well as her rival. She knocked on the door. The laughter stopped. She knocked again.

'Who's there?'

'Me.'

Me. Me. Me ... Pushplata was full of this 'me', and for the first time she felt as if she too had an identity of her own, a personality of her own, separate from Radhika. In that moment, she turned from a shadow into a woman. And she smiled...

The door opened. Yawning and rubbing her eyes, Radhika looked at her, and this time she couldn't ignore her. For in those moments, Pushplata's personality had taken shape and solidified.

'What is it?'

This was a question from one woman to another.

'Where is Ramnath?'

This too was a question from one woman to another.

Both women looked into each other's eyes. For a moment there was a tussle, and then Radhika gave in. She lost her cool. But this had no effect on Pushplata. Radhika asked what Ramnath could possibly be doing in her bedroom so late at night. And having said this, she tried closing the door, but Pushplata barged in, and for the first time Radhika felt scared and Ramnath, hiding in the bathroom, stopped being Dharmendra and became plain old Ramnath again. Pushplata said that Ramnath should not go out without informing anyone. Because there might be errands to run at any time ... And at that moment, Phandaji arrived. When the hero and the starlet had disappeared into the bedroom, Phandaji could scarcely have narrated the story to the sofas and walls. So, he'd got up and left. The watchman had told him that bibiji was already home. He had thought everyone would be asleep. Which is why he didn't ring the bell and quietly opened the door, because he knew that the slightest sound would wake Radhika up. But seeing the bedroom light made him worry – Radhika being up so late was a sign of trouble. Meaning she'd no doubt be lying in bed and wondering about him and the heroine. Meaning the night would end up in a mahabharat. This habit of Radhika's filled him with something approaching panic – how was he supposed to explain that the smile he bestowed upon any girl was purely social in nature, and that to imbue it with greater meaning was improper? Or that if, at a party, the heroine's sister, or the young and beautiful, or not so beautiful, industrialist's daughter who aspired to become a heroine kept chatting him up, that wasn't his fault ... The light in the bedroom didn't bode well. But it was his bedroom – where else could he go? Braving the impending danger, plastering a silly smile across his face, he went into the room and immediately realized something else was amiss.

'What's the matter?' he asked.

Phanda Patialvi was one of those Punjabis who spoke in Punjabi with film producers but in Hindi at home, because he considered Punjabi a rustic, unsophisticated language. He would proudly call himself an Urdu-wallah. He would hold forth on Iqbal and Ghalib. He never bothered to meet Amrita Pritam. He invited Jagannath 'Azad' for dinner...

'Arre, how come you're home so early?' Radhika was smiling. Phanda Patialvi couldn't believe his eyes.

'Early? It's three in the morning.' Phandaji looked at his watch. 'Twelve minutes past three to be precise.' He gave the exact time and then began feeling the pressure in his bladder. When he'd left the hero's place, he'd thought he'd take a leak the moment he reached home. He remembered that he needed to pee, and all but leapt towards the bathroom.

The bathroom door was latched from the inside. He turned around. Both Radhika and Pushplata were looking at him. His hand was poised on the door handle, and he was trying to figure out what one should do if the bathroom door was latched from the inside and one's wife and young daughter were standing in the bedroom looking at the door.

'Oh yes,' he said, as if he'd just remembered something, and walked back. But no one was fooled by the ploy. He decided to ignore this. 'Pushpi, I met that friend of yours at the party, what was her name...'

He looked at Radhika for help. But no help was forthcoming. She stood silently, gnawing at her nails. He turned to Pushplata and asked again, 'What was her name?'

'Why don't you go to the bathroom first?' Pushplata said heartlessly. 'I need to talk to you about a few things.'

'What's the matter? What's the hurry about going to the bathroom?' He tried to find a way out.

But Pushplata wasn't concerned about a way out. So she said nothing. She just kept looking at Phanda Patialvi. Poor Phanda had no reply for Pushplata's gaze. He had never created such a situation in any of his stories. The truth was that the bathroom had never made an appearance in any of his films. He was of the view that peering into a commode on the pretext of being realistic was disgusting. Fearful about the response of the women in the audience, he never even allowed the hero to get too close to the heroine. If the producers insisted, he would insert a dream sequence. After all, one had no control over one's thoughts. Even a stable hand at the Buckingham Palace could dream of Queen Elizabeth. That's why, when Phanda Patialvi had to face a bathroom in real life, his head began to spin.

'All right,' he said. 'I may as well go. To the bathroom. Get me a glass of water in the meantime. I'm really thirsty.'

Pushplata pretended she hadn't heard him.

Utter silence descended upon the room.

Phanda Patialvi had no choice but to go to the bathroom door. This time, the door opened. He went inside. He looked neither left nor right, but went straight to the washbasin and began to gargle. He could see Ramnath clearly in the mirror in front of him ... Phanda Patialvi came out of the bathroom, wiping his face with a towel.

'Yes, Pushpi, so what did you want to tell me?'

'Nothing,' Pushplata said.

No one said anything more. Pushplata left. Phandaji was alone with Radhika.

'I'm feeling very sleepy,' Phandaji said, and lay down on the bed. He turned his face towards the wall.

Ramnath quietly slipped out of the room. He glanced at Phandaji lying in bed, face resolutely turned away. He looked at Radhika who blew him a silent kiss. He shut the bedroom door behind him softly. But when he reached his own bed, he was startled to find Pushplata lying there. He looked at her in panic.

'And if sahib or bai turn up?' he said, looking over his shoulder.

'So what?' Pushplata said.

'If they see us, what will they say?'

'What did he say when he saw you in the bathroom?'

Ramnath had no answer to this question. And since he had no answer, he lay down next to Pushplata and began thinking about those Kanpuri obscenities.

After that night, Ramnath became bolder. He was Phandaji's servant, but now he began calling the shots to some extent. Phandaji's problem was that he didn't have all of Ramnath's 'original' stories yet. A film based on one of his stories was about to release next week, and he didn't want Ramnath to be in any other home at that time. He knew that the moment Ramnath left him, he would be snapped up by some film writer or a hero-writer.

Ramnath was in a relaxed, easy space now. But indulging in the Radhika-Kanpur fantasy every now and then was one thing, doing it day and night was another. On top of that, Pushplata's demands were increasing ... She had stopped being the least bit shy in front of her mother. She would tease him and gesture for him to come to her room. Naturally, Radhika could do little more than stay silent and burn with jealousy...

Around the time all of this was going on, Lisa had already met Ramnath. He liked her. And he wanted to save something of himself for her. He didn't tell Lisa about any of his shenanigans. But she had been pestering him for a long time to start working for her bai – the lady who was her employer – because she needed someone to do a bit of light housework. Ramnath knew that this was something he excelled at. He was also getting tired of Pushplata and Radhika. So, when a friend of his happened to run away from Kanpur and come to Bombay, Ramnath took him to Phandaji and said, 'Sethji, this is Ghaffar Kanpuri, he's an even better story writer than I am...' And Ghaffar Kanpuri began working in Phandaji's house, while Ramnath went away to Midha sahib's.

Lisa liked Ramnath, but her mother Mrs D'Souza

was a strict Catholic and couldn't bear the thought of her daughter going around with some Hindu boy from Kanpur. That's why Ramnath became Peter Singh. Lisa taught him how to make the sign of the cross and say 'amen'. On Sundays, he would put on a suit and go to church with her. In the beginning, he would have to massage his knees for a long time after church. But he was ready to sacrifice this much for Lisa.

He often met Ghaffar Kanpuri in the market. Phandaji had named him Ram Manohar so that the people in his building wouldn't object to the fact that he had hired a Muslim. So, from Ghaffar Kanpuri he became Ram Manohar Kanpuri. He had clearly told Phandaji that he didn't mind any name but he had to remain a Kanpuri, and Phandaji had no objection to this.

Ghaffar Kanpuri, aka Ram Manohar Kanpuri, fully supplanted Ramnath in the house. But Ghaffar was smarter. He also remembered more Kanpuri obscenities. So he earned more too. Ramnath had not taken any salary from Radhika, but Ghaffar didn't see any reason why he should work for free.

With great relish, he would tell Ramnath stories of everything that was happening in the house. He genuinely liked Pushplata. 'What a girl, yaar!' he would say. 'How she bounces about like a cloth ball!' He was planning to run away with her. Ramnath advised him not to do anything so foolish, because while Pushplata underwrote his expenses now, if he ran away with her, he would have to support her. Have you gone crazy, dickhead? But Ghaffar really had become a crazy dickhead ... Then something strange happened, which forced Ghaffar to postpone his plans.

It so happened that a Madhosh sahib lived in Kaanch Bhawan Cooperative Housing Society, across the road from Phandaji. He wrote stories for films and spent the rest of his time in religious activities, doing namaz and keeping rozas. He lived in his house with one servant, three daughters, one wife, and two Filmfare trophies. His servant's name was Abdul Hasan. Everyone called him Abdul.

Madhosh sahib was a strict Muslim. He didn't eat anything that had been touched by a Hindu. He considered it impure. He never ate in a hotel because he couldn't be sure if the meat there was halal or jhatka. Which was why Abdul was very important. Then one day, it was discovered that Abdul's real name was Murarilal. His father's name was Ghanshyam Prasad, and his mother's name was Rukmini. Meaning, he came from a Hindu family. The worst hit was Madhosh sahib's eldest daughter, Alia, who was deeply religious. She wasn't the least bit afraid of Hindus. During the elections, she'd worked for the Muslim League. But she discovered the truth at a time when she couldn't do anything about it. At that time, she was not a Muslim girl, merely a young girl who had given money to Abdul to book a room in Caesar's Palace where she had gone straight from college and where she had been alone with him...

When she found out that Abdul was not a Muslim, it was as if the ground moved beneath her feet and, head spinning, she fell into Abdul's arms ... Abdul who was actually Murarilal.

Now if this Murarilal had been as smart as Ramnath or Ghaffar Kanpuri, nothing would have happened. But he went around telling all the servants of the society that Muslim girls were something else. Many servants got a taste of Alia through Murarilal, and agreed that Muslim girls were indeed quite special. But now Ram Manohar, aka Ghaffar Kanpuri, was in a quandary. Islam was in danger. So when he, through Murarilal, aka Abdul, got a chance to have a go at Alia, he strangled her.

Chaos broke out.

Ram Manohar Kanpuri was arrested. His photograph was published in the next day's newspapers. Journalists assumed it was a matter of love and jealousy. Different journalists wrote different stories. Alia's pictures were published and so were her sisters'. The result was that some producers signed both her younger sisters as heroines. Madhosh sahib himself got a lot of new films...

The day the case began, apart from many other people from the building, Sarla and Rama also turned up in court, because Ram Manohar was Peter's friend, and Peter was Sarla's servant. Naturally, their sympathies lay with Ram Manohar Kanpuri.

'Your name?' the public prosecutor asked.

'Abdul Ghaffar, son of Abdul Jabbar Kanpuri...'

Phandaji was flustered.

Radhika was shocked.

Pushplata broke into peals of laughter and was evicted from the court.

'Did you murder Alia bai?'

'I did, sahib.'

'Why?'

'What could I do, sahib? Were all the Muslim men dead that she had to fuck Hindus...'

I, Rahi Masoom, seek your permission to enter the

story here. All the characters in this story are imaginary and have no connection with contemporary Indian society. In case anyone finds a glimpse of himself or a friend, I apologize. But I am not Allah mian – I can't create characters. I observe the characters around me and mould them to fit my stories. The truth is that I did not even want to talk about Ghaffar Kanpuri or Murarilal. But if they break open the door and force their way into the story, what can I do? Characters are much more powerful than the writer. Come now, let's return to Midha sahib's kitchen.

... Ramnath, aka Peter, put his hand inside Lisa's blouse, and she laughed and slapped it away.

'What are you doing, man!'

'I was just checking to see if everything was okay,' Ramnath said. 'You can't trust those people sitting outside. Tell me clearly – when are you going to marry me? I haven't come here because of your blouse. There were not one but two blouses in Phandaji's flat. And your mother, she's showing no signs of planning to die anytime soon...'

Lisa placed her hand on Ramnath's lips and he kissed it. He had learnt all this from watching Hindi films.

'If you marry me, where will you keep me?'

'In my heart,' Ramnath said, thumping his chest.

'Where will I go to the bathroom?'

Ramnath had no answer to this question. Flustered, he lapsed into silence and then, to hide his embarrassment, he kissed Lisa. Lisa responded but didn't forget practical matters in the heat of their embraces. Again, she asked, 'After we marry, where will you keep me...?'

The truth was that Ramnath was in no mood to get married. He hadn't come to Bombay to marry Lisa. He had come to become a film star ... And if not a film star, a writer. Lisa was just a cup of tea. To take a sip or two from when he wanted to relax. But he couldn't tell her this. So, he put his arms around her neck and said, 'Darling, just give me the order. I'll book a two-bedroom flat...'

That's why, when Rama saw Ramnath at Sursingar one day, while pouring tea from a thermos for Manchandani, she was shocked.

'What are you doing here?' she all but yelled. Sarla was sure to be looking for him, and here he was, loafing about. For a short while, Ramnath heard her out in silence. Then, tilting his head, he said, 'I've booked a flat, bai!'

It was as if Rama was hit by a bolt of lightning. How was it possible that Sarla's servant had booked a flat in the same building as her? Manchandani made a face at Ramnath.

Ramnath saw none of this. He was drunk on the idea of buying a flat. Simpering, he said, 'Behenji, that's...'

Rama was in shock.

'Shut up!' she said angrily. 'Since when did I become your sister?' She turned to Manchandani. 'Ki rab di shaan...' Rama gave a long lecture on everything that was wrong with the times, which were definitely worse than Keshav's. Young women had only called him 'baba'. And here was her friend's servant calling her 'behenji'. And not just that. He was standing in front of her, smiling. So, brandishing the sword of her lecture, Rama cut Ramnath to pieces.

But Ramnath continued to stand in front of her, smiling.

'I write for films, behenji...' he said.

Rama's eyes widened in shock. Ramnath understood that she didn't believe him and so he pulled out his Film Writers Association card from his pocket and showed it to her. That was when Rama Chopra learned that he had actually sold three stories.

This is what had happened. After Ramnath left, Phanda Patialvi was in a soup. Before Ramnath had arrived on the scene, he used to write different kinds of stories. His position in the marketplace wasn't what it used to be. He was worried about what would happen a couple of years down the line. And he couldn't figure a way out. That's when Ramnath appeared like a gift from god and, all of a sudden, Phanda Patialvi's storytelling style changed. Important directors, producers and producer-directors began running after him. Their imported cars were parked outside his house at all hours of the day. And once again, Phandaji began dropping names from the film industry in front of all and sundry.

'What can I say, BR is not willing to let go of me under any circumstance ... I told Dilip Kumar yesterday that it's time for him to retire ... Raj-ji, I mean Raj Kapoor sir, he can't get by with Khwaja sahib's work now ... But, sahib, I'm a human being, not a machine, I can't just keep churning out stories...'

That's why Phanda Patialvi was ready to endure anything. Who could know what was happening in his house anyway? He was also bored of his wife. And because of Ramnath, he was spared that labour too

... And the truth was that it was when Ramnath was with him that he wrote his most popular novel, *Saanch ki Aanch*. Many critics observed that in this day and age, when one could only hear the sound of values breaking in every corner, Phandaji, by writing *Saanch ki Aanch*, had fulfilled his duty to society. A man can't live on bread alone. He needs values to make his life worthwhile, and Phandaji, by pushing characters to the background and making values and principles his true heroes, had shown a courage that modern critics couldn't ignore...

Both Pushplata and Radhika laughed openly at *Saanch ki Aanch*. But their laughter stayed inside the flat...

In short, Phandaji couldn't manage without Ramnath. And Lisa had whisked Ramnath away. At first, he was happy, because he found the sight of Ramnath smiling at Pushplata abhorrent. There was also some tension in the house because of the Pushplata-Radhika-Ramnath triangle. There was a tug of war between Pushplata and Radhika, as each one tried to outdo the other in generosity and magnanimity to win Ramnath over. Naturally, the burden of this generosity was borne by Phandaji's income ... That's why, at first, he was grateful that Ramnath was gone. But when he began narrating a story to a producer, he suddenly felt as if he was reverting to his old style.

'Can I say something?' the producer said. 'This story doesn't have that feel, it's not juicy enough…'

For Phandaji, the penny dropped. And he came to the conclusion that he just couldn't work without his wife's lover. Writing *Saanch ki Aanch* was fine. But what producers wanted were stories by Ramnath, middle school pass (or fail). And he had also promised an upcoming star that he'd produce a film with him as the hero – with the caveat that the young man would have to marry Pushplata. He needed some seven and a half lakh rupees for the film and the wedding, and he couldn't make this much without Ramnath's help. And so, the Phanda-Nathan team was born.

The world of Hindi films is a world of incomplete people. Here, when two people come together, they don't multiply. They become one. Shankar-Jaikishan, Laxmikant-Pyarelal, Kalyanji-Anandji, Salim-Javed, Sapan-Jagmohan, Faiz-Salim, Majid-Narvi-Girish … Two becoming one was a proper tradition. This reaches absurd heights when someone can't find another person to join him and decides to mask his solo status by repeating his own name. Shyamji-Ghanshyamji.

But in the era we are talking about, duos were commonplace only in the world of Hindi film music. Phandaji launched the first writer duo, and the English weekly *Screen* published a full-page article announcing this along with a Phanda-Ramnath photograph. It was as if an earthquake had hit the Hindi film world...

Phanda's partner could hardly work as Midha sahib's cook. So, Phandaji advised Ramnath to leave the job and gave him a one-bedroom flat in Khar. Later, he decided to give the flat to his son-in-law to-be and even promised him as much. That's when he transferred the flat he had booked for himself in Sursingar to Ramnath, and that's how Rama met Ramnath there.

'What did you say you do?' a stunned Rama asked.

'Film writer,' Ramnath said. He knew Rama wouldn't believe him. And why just Rama, no one would believe that a cook had become a writer. That's why Ramnath had insisted that *Screen* publish his photograph. He always carried a copy in his pocket, and now he took it out to show Rama.

Ramnath had already decided that it wouldn't look good if he met Sarla or a friend of hers, or Midha or a friend of his at a party and if any of them let slip that he used to be a cook. So, he had thought up a story for himself along the lines of the film *Ram aur Shyam*. This story was also about twin brothers. Peter, who used to cook at Sarla's house, was Ramnath's brother. When he'd told Phandaji, Phandaji had jumped with excitement, calling it a 'golden-jubilee idea'.

So Ramnath decided to try out this golden-jubilee idea on Rama. He said, 'Behenji, I think you're mistaking me for Shyamnath, known as Peter, who used to work as a cook...'

Desperate to save her dignity, Rama was ready to believe anything. If this man was not the Peter who used to cook in Sarla's house, what was the harm in having him for a neighbour? Actually, since Sarla was away at her mother's place, Rama hadn't met her for about two months and had no idea that Peter didn't work there anymore. Sarla had returned that very day, and before Ramnath turned up, Rama had been telling Manchandani how Sarla had returned that very day and how she hadn't been able to go to the station and how Sarla would quarrel with her because she hadn't...

'You look so alike.' She laughed as she poured tea for Ramnath from the thermos. She thought she should become friendly with him right away so that it would be easy for her to get invitations to muhurats and premieres later.

So, Rama got down to the business of becoming friends with Ramnath. Bored, Manchandani began reading *Screen* and discovered many things about the Phanda-Nathan duo. Gujarati-Marathi-Hindi-English journalist Pancharan Mishra had turned Ramnath into Ramanathan and had cooked up his entire life story. Manchandani discovered that, because of his father's sudden death, Ramanathan had been unable to take his MA exam. The memory of his university days still filled Ramanathan with sadness. The glory of those tennis lawns, the revelries of the drama club. Ramanathan had been interested in acting since childhood. His father had also been fond of acting, in fact, his father had been the lead actor of a well-known theatre group in Uttar Pradesh ... Ramnath knew every word was a lie, but Pancharan Mishra had assured him that this was normal in the film world. Everyone knew it was lies. But everyone had had similar things written about them, so no one bothered to check the truth. Pancharan Mishra had even worked out a list of Ramnath's favourite writers on his own. After reading the *Screen* article, Phandaji informed him that among playwrights, he was a devotee of Shakespeare and Ibsen. Among novelists, he loved Balzac and Tolstoy. Among poets, he liked Keats's melancholy and Goethe's grave observations … Pancharan Mishra was careful to name only those writers and poets who were unlikely to have ever been read by film folk, but whose names cropped up in conversations every now and then. It was only when Hindustani theatre adapted Ibsen's *Charlie's Aunt* as *Khalid ki Khala*, that film folk discovered that there was someone besides Shakespeare who wrote plays. They discovered Bernard Shaw after the release of *My Fair Lady*, but Ibsen remained special. The names of his plays had been memorized and, indeed, some stars spoke about him with such familiarity as if *they* had written the plays. Keeping all this in mind, Pancharan Mishra had stuck Ibsen's name into the interview. Pancharan Mishra was of the opinion that if any writer narrated even a lousy story to Sudip Kumar, Balraj Kapur, Vrajendra or Ramesh Khanna, saying that it was based on Ibsen, these people would instantly say 'yes' to the story and the writer could demand whatever fee he wanted from the producer. In Bombay, it wasn't the story that sold, it was the hero's assent. Pancharan Mishra had deliberately not included any Indian writers among Ramnath's favourites because that would be damaging to his interests. But when it came to favourite actors, Pancharan Mishra went with Indian names. Ramnath even spoke out against some stars who were on their way down, to cultivate the image of an outspoken man who did not believe in sucking up to people…

Manchandani was very impressed by Ramnath.

'How do you people think up stories?' he asked.

Ramnath laughed. 'Writing a story isn't difficult. Just pick up a pen and start writing.'

This was beyond Manchandani's comprehension. He was going to ask another question when Ramnath took out a tin of 555 cigarettes and extended it towards him. Manchandani had just graduated from beedis to Charminars. It was the first time in his life that he had been in such close proximity to a tin of 555s. He took one cigarette. Ramnath lit it with a gold lighter and then lit one for himself.

'But how do you people figure out what will happen in a story, how the events will take place one after the other?' Manchandani asked after taking a long drag.

Ramnath laughed again.

Pancharan Mishra had told Ramnath that if he didn't understand a particular question, or didn't know the answer, he should just laugh, because then the person asking the question would feel that he'd asked something so foolish it could only be dismissed with laughter. But Pancharan Mishra had also made him mug up the answers to several important questions. Naturally, all the money being spent was Phandaji's. And it had been decided that ten per cent of all earnings would go to Pancharan Mishra. Sixty per cent would go to Phandaji, and thirty to Ramnath. Pancharan Mishra had also made himself Ramnath's secretary. He wasn't going to take a salary for this, just 300 rupees towards expenses for his car. What Ramnath didn't know was that Pancharan Mishra wanted to get Phanda Patialvi out of the way and install himself as his partner. That's why he was working overtime to boost Ramnath's image.

Pancharan Mishra had come from Ahmedabad to become a film writer. But things didn't work out. He thought he had a collection of fantastic stories. But when writers like Premchand, Yashpal, Bhagwaticharan, Ali Abbas Husaini, Krishan Chander, Bedi, Manto and Ismat Chughtai had lost out to Pandit Sudarshan, Bharat Vyas, Shams Lakhnavi, etc., what chance did Pancharan Mishra have? Still, he didn't lose hope. He couldn't become a film writer, so he became a film journalist because, after all, what was the harm? But when that too didn't work out, he began working in public relations. He began fixing Filmfare awards. He acquired a flat, a car, a wife and children, and a respectable bank balance. But a splinter still pricked his heart, a painful reminder that what he really wanted to be was a writer. So when Phandaji introduced him to Ramnath, he saw the hidden talent there and decided after his very first meeting that, all this while in Bombay, he had merely been waiting for Ramnath. He began imparting skills to Ramnath, and like a good student, Ramnath began following his instructions. He looked at Manchandani and laughed in a way that made Manchandani blush.

'The thing is,' Ramnath began, 'the writer first has to decide whether the story should be a tragedy or have a happy ending. Then he thinks about the hero, whether the hero should be a labourer or doctor or dacoit. Once all this is decided, everything becomes extremely simple…'

Manchandani nodded as if to say he had understood everything, though he hadn't understood a thing. He didn't have the guts to ask the same question a third time, so he focussed on finishing his cigarette as quickly as possible so that he could light another 555. But Ramnath caught on and put the tin of cigarettes back in his pocket. Irritated, Manchandani was about to ask another question, but at that moment, Bholanath Khatak landed up and Rama said –

'I have to tell you something really interesting...'

At first, Bholanath found it impossible to believe this 'really interesting' piece of information, because the man sitting in front of him was clearly Peter. But when he saw the photograph in *Screen*, he was stunned and had to admit that there could be a *Ram aur Shyam* in real life too, whether Dilip Kumar was acting in it or not.

Bholanath Khatak – without any real reason – considered himself an expert on films. He had no legitimate or illegitimate connection with films, but because his older brother, Shobhanath Chopra, had married film star Rajnibala's stepsister, he felt he had a close family relationship with the Hindi film world, and spoke about Hindi films with such authority as if he'd made dozens of them himself.

So Bholanath Khatak looked at Ramnath and smiled. Ramnath smiled back, though in his heart of hearts he was cursing him with the choicest abuses. Because though he was a writer now, how could he forget that this bastard, along with Midha, was always looking for a chance to touch Lisa?

Like everyone else, Bholanath also believed that there was no better writer on earth than him. Stories began crawling in his brain like worms the moment he met Ramnath, and he began dreaming in flash forward mode:

His stories were selling for one lakh, two lakhs, indeed why just one or two lakhs, they were selling for seven lakhs, eight lakhs. He had a ten-bedroom bungalow on the beach, with one wife, three lovers, eight servants, two maidservants, four cars…

And so Ramnath and Bholanath Khatak became friends. The truth is, Bholanath firmly believed that mixing with the lower orders was a bad thing. But he thought of himself as an intellectual, and in his heart of hearts he decided that he'd become thick with Ramnath and use him to turn his own stories into scripts, then sit back contentedly – plus he would get the opportunity to meet Waheeda Rehman.

Rama had no idea that Bholanath was secretly in love with Waheeda Rehman. Without mentioning her name, he would get Rama to do her hair like Waheeda. He tried to make her wear Waheeda-like clothes. When he slept with Rama once or twice a month, he would imagine her to be Waheeda while he became Guru Dutt. He was convinced that Waheeda had been involved with Guru Dutt and said as much to his friends, as if he'd heard this from Guru Dutt himself.

... With Ramnath's help, he could sell a story too, but he had stubbornly decided to set a condition – only if Waheeda was the heroine would he part with his story. He had already chosen one for the film. Arre, that story in which the villain rapes the heroine and she gets pregnant and then the hero, to save the heroine from scandal, marries her and they begin living together happily. He was even willing to play the villain – the very thought made the blood rush to his temples, and he sat back with one leg crossed over the other.

All too often, Bholanath had to cross one leg over the other, and that's why he thought that any man who saw Rama would also do the same, and this was unbearable to him. There were fights between husband and wife. Rama would threaten suicide, but instead, she would tie a rakhi at Rakshabandhan on the man concerned, and Khatakji would breathe a sigh of relief. But then he would see Rama talk cordially to someone else, and the mahabharat would begin all over again.

Rama was a simple woman. She hadn't realized until

now why Sarla always stuck to her. Sometimes she would mind, but she would console herself with the fact that Sarla was useful to her too. More than money, the biggest advantage was that she had started accompanying Sarla to the kinds of homes she could never have dreamt of going to on her own ... She discovered Sarla's reality only much later. She remembered her college days and, terrified, stopped meeting Sarla altogether. That's when Bholanath Khatak began taunting her about Sarla.

Ali Amjad lived in number two and Khatakji in number one.

Actually, it would be wrong to say that Bholanath lived in number one. More than him, his telephone lived in number one. He was like a snake guarding its treasure, that is, the telephone. Apart from his height and his telephone, there was nothing big about Bholanath. But because of these two things, he considered himself bigger than every other resident of Sursingar.

He used the story of his friendship with the Raja of Satna to build his image. No man in the neighbourhood could swear on Gangajal or the Quran that he knew anything about it. But Bholanath Khatak would seize any opportunity that came his way to bring up the topic of his friendship with the Raja sahib of Satna – so much so that every resident of Sursingar eventually knew the story by heart.

Yes, Rama never spoke openly of the friendship. But sometimes she would drop a few subtle hints that if the princess of Satna hadn't fallen head over heels in love with her Nath, the friendship would never have ended. At this, Khatakji would put up such a convincing act of being shy and embarrassed that even great actors like Dilip Kumar would have conceded defeat. He would tell his wife, 'Rama, how many times have I told you not to say such things. People might believe them…'

Bholanath never made such statements in Punjabi, it was either in Hindi or English, so that people could understand every word. By doing so, he wanted to prove to everyone that he had indeed had a dalliance with the princess of Satna. Actually, on such occasions, he didn't speak much Hindi either – he believed that the mother tongue of all educated people in India was English.

Despite all this, no one in the neighbourhood actually believed the alleged love story. But the story fed Bholanath's ego, and because the residents of Sursingar needed to use the telephone, they had no option but to endure listening to the story again and again. Also, Khatakji fancied himself a bit of a handsome fellow.

Rama too was more or less in agreement with this view – she thought he was magnificent.

Apart from Bholanath and Rama, there were also a daughter and two sons in the family. Mita, the daughter, was married and lived in Jalandhar. Her husband had a business in old cars, but Bholanath and Rama had told everyone in the neighbourhood that Mishrilal, Mita's husband, was soon going to open a car manufacturing factory. And his cars would be a thousand times better than Sanjay Gandhi's Maruti, which was why Indira Gandhi was putting obstructions in his path every single day. Maruti was singled out because Bholanath thought that opposing Indira Gandhi was the current fad, and he always liked to be up-to-date on such things. He had no understanding of politics. But he read the *Times of India* every day, and if he found some sucker in the evening, he would pour himself some Black Knight or Diplomat whisky from Chivas Regal bottles and bore the hell out of the other person by lecturing him on politics. He would speak with such authority as if he had grown up playing with Nixon and Brezhnev, and Chou En-lai was his childhood buddy. Ilson-Wilson, eGaulle-deGaulle, Aadat-Saadat, Ito-Tito – he considered them all unworthy of his time. And as for the policies of the government in Delhi, he spoke about them in such a manner as if Indira Gandhi was the prime minister in name only and he was the real architect of those policies. Rama would keep agreeing with him, and the two boys, sitting close by, would keep nodding. But Mita was a bit blunt and outspoken. If she got fed up with Bholanath's flights of fancy, she would tick him off. That's why, deep inside, Khatakji was a little wary of Mita. Rama herself had confided this to Mrs Verma.

The thing was, whenever Rama was sulking or cross with Bholanath, she would go to some woman or the other in the building and talk her ear off. And she was cross with Bholanath every second or third day.

She loved nicking money from Bholanath. Whenever she got an opportunity, she would rifle through his pockets. She tried to teach Mita to do the same to her husband, but Mita turned out to be a poor student. She paid no attention to her mother's advice. But Rama kept at her thieving assiduously. Most of the time, Bholanath never found out, because Rama was clever – if there were 25 rupees, she would take 4, and if there were 40 rupees and 70 paise, she would take only 7 rupees and 30 paise. If Bholanath did bring it up, she would make fun of him. What kind of theft was this? Why would a thief leave behind more money than he stole? Bholanath knew someone had taken the money, but he could think of no way to counter Rama. He would swallow his annoyance. But he would stay alert. He would count the money in his pocket and write down the amount in a diary – all this to trip Rama up. And then he would come down on her like a ton of bricks. They would fight and curse each other all night. Bholanath would curse in English and Hindi, but Rama, who had no interest in asserting any kind of superiority over anyone, would speak in Punjabi. And she would respond with equal vehemence … As a result, Ali Amjad's little nephew learnt a whole lot of Punjabi abuses and sometimes, just for a lark, he would put his arms around his uncle's neck and call him 'harami da puttar'. Perturbed, Ali Amjad would tell Seema, 'What is going on? If Wassu has to be taught how to curse, at least teach him some proper swear words. This "harami da puttar" is so unbecoming.' But what could they do? In an attempt to send a message to Bholanath, one day Amjad told him a story.

Apparently, when Firaq Gorakhpuri visited Bombay, many bigwigs from the film industry threw a party for him. Now it is a strange coincidence, but all the Hindi film bigwigs are either Punjabi or Bengali. The Bengalis had no interest in Firaq Gorakhpuri. So, all the big Punjabi stars gathered at the party. B.R. Chopra, Dilip Kumar, Vinod Khanna, Shammi Kapoor ... Firaq sahib was feeling left out. Everybody was speaking to each other in Punjabi. Firaq sahib listened to them for a while, rolling his eyes. Then he said to Dilip Kumar, 'Yusuf, I think I may as well learn Punjabi.' Yusuf sahib replied in all seriousness, 'No, Firaq sahib, why do you need to learn Punjabi?' To this, Firaq sahib said, 'Bhai, I'm old, I'm getting to the age when I'm likely to die. My entire life has been spent committing all kinds of sins. I will obviously go to hell. I may as well learn its official language, it'll help me once I'm there.'

Bholanath laughed uproariously at this, then took out a cigarette from Amjad's tin and busied himself lighting it with a matchstick. Amjad retrieved his cigarettes and fled back to his flat. He told Harish, 'Yaar, this Khatak is a strange creature.'

Harish said, 'I keep telling you, find another house.'

Amjad said, 'Where shall I look? I found even this flat with such difficulty.'

And he was right. He had found this flat with great difficulty. The thing is, Bombay and houses are two distinct entities. No one knows whether you will find god in this city, but you will certainly never find a house. Perhaps because you can't smuggle a flat from Dubai or Abu Dhabi. And a factory to make fake houses is yet to open in Ulhasnagar. That is to say, for a middle-class Muslim like Ali Amjad, finding a house in Bombay was about as difficult as finding Allah. Even god might not be able to differentiate between a Sindhi and someone from Uttar Pradesh, but a Bombay landlord could spot this fine difference. Bombay's graveyards don't lag behind its landlords either. They too can differentiate between Shia-Sunni, Hanafi-Wahabi, Shia-Khoja. In Bombay, you can find neither house nor grave with ease. Ali Amjad had no experience of looking for a grave, but he had indeed looked for a house in Bombay.

Ali Amjad was a good man, but when it came to houses, he had many flaws. The first flaw was that he was a Muslim. The second was that he worked in films. The third was that he was not a Khoja or Catholic or Sindhi. But he still required a house. That's why he had refused to let go of Tolaram, the broker.

'Come, Amzadji,' Tolaram said with a grin, pronouncing 'j' as 'z'.

'I come every day, sahib,' Amjad said.

Tolaram laughed. 'That was like a filmy dialogue!' he said, then scratched his thigh and began gazing at his typist. Every time he scratched himself, he stared at his typist, because he believed that the pleasure of scratching increased manifold if he looked at her. After scratching himself about twenty times, he said, 'Yesterday my wife said, why don't you narrate that story of yours to Amzad bhai? Hell, it's a first-class subject. I've shoved in three bloody rape scenes. The first bloody rape is of the hero's sister...'

'Let's talk about the house first, Tolaramji.'

'Arre, the house is all yours Amzad bhai! Just listen to the beginning. It is evening. The opening credits have gone...'

'Where's the flat?'

'Here. In Bandra. The heroine is in a bikini, imagine it's Saira Banu. Such legs she has...' Looking at his typist, he began scratching his thigh again.

Ali Amjad persisted, 'How big is the flat?'

'Eight hundred square feet.'

After he finished scratching, Tolaram continued with his story, 'When the waiter sees the heroine, he bloody starts stammering. Now imagine V. Gopal as the waiter.

You just have to look at his bloody face and you feel like laughing…'

'How much deposit?'

'The usual, three months. My wife said to me, tell Amzad bhai he can narrate the story in his own name. She's become your bloody fan. We can go fifty-fifty.'

'Let's go and have a look at the flat.'

'But don't tell the landlord you are a film writer,' Tolaram said, getting up. 'Bloody people don't give houses to film-wallahs. Bloody people believe that if they give their houses to film-wallahs, the honour of their daughters and daughters-in-law will be in danger. As if their daughters' and daughters-in-law's honour is stored away like pickle when film-wallahs don't stay in the same building. Arre, it's all bloody nonsense, Amzad bhai! I have a lot of stories about such daughters and daughters-in-law. Arre, Amzad bhai, what I'm saying is that the Amzad-Tolaram team can send the Salim-Javed team packing!'

'I think the Tola-Masha team would be much better than the Amzad-Tola team,' Ali Amjad said.

Tolaram laughed uproariously. His typist looked at him and smiled. Tolaram winked at her. 'Miss

Fernandez's destiny will change if we team up. She'll bloody enjoy typing the rape scenes...'

'Ah, you're impossible!' Miss Fernandez said with a laugh.

Tolaram laughed again. 'What name did you say? Tolaram-Masharam...'

His laughter had no effect on his typist, who was in a hurry to go home. Outside, at the bus stop, a fat Khoja woman was bent over, scratching her calf. Behind her, a coconut-seller was slicing off a coconut's bristly coir. A beautiful girl in a miniskirt passed by Tolaram's ground-floor office. The fat Khoja woman straightened up and began scratching her stomach.

'Let's go, Amzad bhai,' Amjad heard Tolaram's voice and, removing his gaze from the street, turned to look at him.

'Let's go.'

'Miss Fernandez,' Tolaram said, 'lock the office and give the key to my wife. Let's go, Amzad bhai...'

Tolaram and Ali Amjad came out into the street. Amjad clambered into the sidecar. Tolaram started the motorcycle.

'Who's the landlord?'

'Sindhi,' Tolaram said. The motorcycle started. And the rest of his words got drowned out in its noise.

The landlord, Motwani, lived in a narrow, crowded lane in Chimbai. He had a bookshop in Colaba where he sold only English books. He smoked only English cigarettes. He was the father of three daughters. He had two flats in Pali Hill's Suryadarshan Housing Society. Both the flats were rented out, and he lived in rented accommodation himself. The two Pali Hill flats fetched him a rent of 2,600 rupees, but he lived in a 2,200-square-foot flat and paid a rent of 97 rupees. Meaning, a monthly saving of 2,503 rupees. Saving was the most important thing. That's why Motwani met the potential tenant of his third flat with a smile.

'Will you have something to drink?'

'Thank you,' Ali Amjad said.

'What newspapers do you write for?'

'*Dharmyug*,' Tolaram said. '*Sarika*, *Saptahik Hindustan*. Just list out all the magazines you know. He writes for all of them.'

'Okay, okay,' Motwani said. 'Tolaram said you were a journalist...'

'No,' Ali Amjad interrupted him. 'I'm not a journalist, I'm a patrakar.'

As he was saying this, Tolaram stretched his hand out and picked up the tin of Dunhills from in front of Motwani. He said, 'Say what you will, Amzad bhai, but there's nothing like British cigarettes.'

'My name has a "j" in it, not a "z".'

Tolaram laughed. 'Have one.' He pushed the tin towards Ali Amjad.

'No, bhai. I will smoke my own cigarettes.' Ali Amjad took out his pack of Charminars.

'I think I saw your name in a film magazine,' Motwani said.

'Arre, and how's that his fault?' Tolaram interrupted. He knew that if this conversation around films continued, he was in danger of losing his six per cent commission. He also knew that despite running a business of books, Motwani was not an educated or well-read man. That's why he added, 'Maybe bhabhiji made a mistake while reading his name.'

'I can give the house on a company lease,' Motwani said.

'I'm a freelancer,' Ali Amjad said.

'No, sahib,' Motwani shook his head. 'I've been stuck in this leave-and-licence situation before.' He looked at

Tolaram. 'You were the one who said one shouldn't do business with film-wallahs or Muslims.'

All the blood in Ali Amjad's body rushed to his face.

'But that tenant was a Punjabi Hindu,' Tolaram said, cursing Motwani inwardly. 'This one is a nationalist Muslim.'

'The thing is, bhai sahib, the housing society doesn't permit any non-Sindhi to rent a house here,' Motwani told Ali Amjad.

'I am a Muslim and I also work in films,' Ali Amjad said. He thought it was necessary for him to say this. He was not a religious man. He didn't believe in Allah. He didn't do namaz. He didn't fast during Ramzan. He was an uncompromising critic of organizations like the Muslim League and the Jamat-e-Islami ... But he was not ashamed of the fact that he had been born into a Muslim family. And he did not want to insult himself or his country by hiding his name and identity.

On their way there, Tolaram had said that they would rent the flat under some other name. But life was far more precious than Tolaram's six per cent commission. You can't live according to your ideals if you change your name...

Ali Amjad turned to look at Tolaram, who in turn was looking at the calendar hanging on the wall in front of him. The calendar advertised toothpowder and had a picture of Saira Banu on it. There was more of her skin on display than clothes ... Tolaram was trying to mentally undress the picture, and was gently scratching his thigh. Realizing that Amjad was looking at him, he bent towards him and said softly, 'Amzad bhai, do you think she uses bloody toothpowder on her teeth,' and started laughing.

With a national-integration type smile plastered on his face, Motwani was waiting for Amjad to look at him so that he could say what he had to say. When Amjad finally did, Motwani said, 'What do I care about your religion, Amzadji, but I am helpless in the face of the society's rules.' Motwani turned the 'j' into 'z' again. 'If you were a Sindhi, I would have certainly given you the flat.'

'But why would I be a Sindhi?' Amjad asked.

Motwani sahib started laughing, as if Amjad had cracked a joke.

'Motwani sahib,' Amjad said, 'I am in desperate need of a house. If you had said become a Hindu, I would have become one, but becoming a Sindhi is beyond me.' The bitter taste in his mouth was suffocating him. He stood up. 'Let's go, Tolaramji...'

And without waiting for Tolaram, he left.

Night was falling in the narrow Chimbai alley. A cool breeze wafted in from the sea. There was a crowd at the corner shop, waiting to buy kerosene. There was a poster of Manoj Kumar's film, *Shor*, on the wall across. Next to it was a big poster with a photograph of Indira Gandhi. She was smiling and inviting members of the Bombay Congress Committee to gather at Chowpatty and listen to her speech.

Looking at Indiraji's pearly white teeth, Ali Amjad was reminded of the toothpowder calendar he'd seen on Motwani's wall, where the emphasis had been more on the legs than on the teeth.

'Don't worry, Amzad bhai,' Tolaram came up to him. 'As long as Tolaram lives, you cannot stay homeless. Just today my wife was telling me that if you want to team up with Amzad bhai, first you have to find him a house. Wait and see, Amzad bhai, now I'll make sure you get a house from none other than a Sindhi.'

Tolaram kept his word.

This flat was also a Sindhi's – Chhattaram Manchandani.

In the very first meeting, Ali Amjad had told him that he was a Muslim and a film writer. It wasn't clear whether Manchandani would give him a flat after hearing this, but Mrs Sadhna Manchandani sealed the deal by asking, 'Bhai sahib, can you get me to meet Dharmendra and Rajesh Khanna?'

'Why not? Sure,' he said.

'Are Dharmendra and Saira Banu really having an affair?' she asked, and Ali Amjad was surprised by her Urdu diction. It turned out that she had once been Khwaja Ahmad Abbas's heroine and he had spent a year working on her Urdu. The film got made but was never released because it didn't have a rape scene, it didn't have a fight between Shetty and the hero ... there wasn't even a Padma Khanna cabaret number. But Sadhna thought of herself as a film heroine, and spoke about movies with such authority as if she was the third generation of her family to act in films. Whenever she heard of a film scandal, she would let out a deep sigh – if her film had been released, there would have been so many scandals involving her too. Pancharan Mishra had worked as her PRO. He had said that if she wanted to become a star, first, she should hide the fact of her marriage and, second, acquire a reputation by linking herself to a famous hero if nothing else. Dharmendra and Rajesh Khanna were both extremely busy, so Pancharan Mishra thought there was no point getting involved with either of them. He chose Chintu Kapoor instead, but Manchandani was not agreeable, and so Sadhna missed becoming a star by a whisker. And from then on, her heart soured towards Manchandani. In a way, she regretted marrying him. He was in the construction business and had nothing to do with film folk. That's why when, in the person of Ali Amjad, she met her first film person a full four-and-a-half years after her marriage, her old wounds reopened. And she began chatting to Ali Amjad as if he was someone from her mother's home. Is Raaj Kumar really bald? Does Dev saab get facelifts? Has Kamal Amrohi really married for the third time? Doesn't Rekha look like she's over thirty? How long will Sharmila and Nawab Pataudi's marriage last? Is Gulzar thinking of romancing Raakhee in order to forget Meena Kumari? Questions, questions, and more questions.

Manchandani saw that he would have to give the Sursingar flat to Ali Amjad. So he quietly raised the rent by fifty rupees, and Tolaram didn't object either, because if the rent went up, so did his commission.

'But be careful about one thing,' Manchandani said after everything had been settled. 'Flat number one is occupied by Bholanath Khatak, a man to steer clear of.'

'If he's in number one, I will have to say hello,' Ali Amjad said.

'Be careful of Rama,' Sadhna said. 'She's a very predatory woman.'

'Rama is Mrs Bholanath,' Manchandani said. 'I saved myself by getting her to tie a rakhi on me.' He started laughing. Mrs Manchandani started laughing. Tolaram started laughing. Ali Amjad didn't laugh because he didn't understand what there was to laugh about.

'But don't forget – you have to get me to meet Rajesh Khanna,' Mrs Manchandani said.

When Ali Amjad promised to do so, he was given the key to flat number two in Sursingar. He couldn't believe that he had actually got the flat. Quickly, he put the key in his pocket and kept holding on to it tightly, as if he was afraid it would disappear if he let go.

When he came down from Manchandani's flat, Tolaram said, 'Listen to my story some day, Amzad bhai.'

'Why not? Sure,' he said.

'I bought some old English novels for fifty rupees,'

Tolaram said confidentially. 'Because if, by god's grace, our partnership takes off, where will we find new stories every day? My wife gave me this idea. She's a wonderful woman. And a BA, first class. I was buying a new novel when the shopkeeper – I got him a flat as well – told me not to buy it, not if I wanted to become a film writer. He said he'd got ten copies and ten writers had bought all of them. He'd ordered ten more. Then he chose some books for me. He didn't let me buy any novel that was less than twenty-five years old. Today's second-rate film writers wouldn't even have heard of the books he picked for me. Last night, my wife started reading one of the novels to me. The first bloody scene was so bloody good that I was stunned. The hero is a police officer, and the heroine is the daughter of the criminal he wants to arrest…'

'We'll sit down one day and do this,' Ali Amjad interrupted him.

'Come, let me drop you to the flat.'

'Arre no,' Ali Amjad hastily said. He was afraid that if Tolaram came with him, he would not stop until he had finished narrating the entire novel.

'Arre, why are you being so formal, Amzad bhai?' Tolaram asked.

'No, bhai. I'll go by myself. Manchandani sahib has already written a letter to the secretary of the society.'

'Don't take people to too many shoots,' said Tolaram. And he laughed strangely. 'Manchandani is busy making money day and night, and poor Sadhna bhabhi has to get by with shoots.'

He laughed again, louder.

The sound of his laughter merged with the sound of his motorcycle.

'We'll meet…' Ali Amjad shouted to him.

Tolaram departed and Ali Amjad was left alone in the forest of local and foreign cars spread out below Pali Hills Apartments.

The news about Ali Amjad becoming a tenant had reached Sursingar even before he got there. The first person he met was Rama. She was lying in wait for him. She was upset with Manchandani for giving his flat to a Muslim. Not one to take chances, she had already found out how many of his films had been released and how many he was currently writing. The Khatak family was an educated family, and educated people know how to hide their bigotry.

Rama believed that she had every right to hate Muslims. And she had this right because her family had to leave Punjab during the turmoil of 1947. They used to lend money at very high interest to Punjabi farmers. When the demand for Pakistan began gathering steam, her family gathered all the pawned jewellery in its possession and came away to Delhi before the riots began. Rama said that her paternal grandfather had tons of gold stashed away. If the partition hadn't happened, her grandfather wouldn't have fled to Delhi with all this wealth. Everyone suffered on account of the partition except him. When he arrived in Delhi, he staked his claim and occupied Abdusamad Khan Bisati's house. And spent the rest of his life in prayer and in cursing Muslims.

In 1947, Rama was twelve-and-a-half years old. By that age, a girl has learnt how to hate and how to love. She didn't fall in love with anyone, but after she came to Delhi, she did start hating Muslims. Hating Muslims had become a sort of fashion in north India in those days. Everyone had the number of people killed in Pakistan on their fingertips, and they were so preoccupied with this arithmetic that they had no time to count the corpses lying on the streets of Hindustan. They believed that only Hindu women had honour and Muslim women just had bodies. But even in those days, there were a few crazy people here and there, on both sides of the border, who screamed themselves hoarse saying that dead bodies and daggers had no religion, and honour had no identity or caste. But Rama didn't have even one such crazy person as her neighbour. That's why no one told Rama that Muslims in India had been killed, just like Hindus in Pakistan. If it was true that:

> Hope floated away like a vessel of unbaked clay
> Sohni was marooned in the midst of a storm

Then this was true too:

> In Jama Masjid was the essence of Allah
> In Chandni Chowk it was always night

But the whole truth was that:

> The song of the five rivers began to burn
> There was no Radha in the land of Krishna
> There was no Sita in the land of Ram
> Heer was paraded naked on the streets
> Every tale of the Raavi was washed away
> Some looters became important men
> And we became refugees in our own homes
> The women set off for the borders

Without their nose-rings
Without even a piece of cloth to cover their heads
Their shoes abandoned at the thresholds of
  their homes
Something big has happened here
Homes have been burnt to create light.

But this truth, this reality was known to very few people. And Rama was not one of them. That's why, when she found out that a Muslim was going to move in next door, she thought that it was Sadhna who had taken it upon herself to upset her. But like most moderately educated middle-class women, Rama was very fond of watching films, conversing in English every now and then, and reading the newspaper. In her heart of hearts, she too wanted to meet Rajesh Khanna, and she thought that by befriending Ali Amjad all her filmy dreams could come true.

Rama always maintained that she fell in love with Bholanath the instant she saw his photograph, but the truth was she fell in love with the fact that Bholanath lived in Bombay. By becoming Mrs Bholanath Chopra, she would get the opportunity to live in Bombay and meet her Dilip Kumars, Dharmendras and Rajeshes. She never said Rajesh Khanna's full name. He was just Rajesh to her. And even if she couldn't meet them, she would be able to breathe the air of the same city where the stars lived, romanced and marched to seek help for flood victims.

But when she arrived in Bombay and discovered that the person she'd always thought of as Dilip Kumar was really Yusuf Khan, she crossed out his name from the list of stars she wanted to meet – 'meet' in much the same way one would 'meet' a god. That left Rajesh and Dharam. And Ali Amjad was writing films for both of them. That's why she set aside her hatred and waited for him to arrive. The moment she heard the slightest sound, she raced to the door and peered through the keyhole ... And that's how the first person Ali Amjad saw in Sursingar was Rama.

When Ali Amjad was opening the lock on flat number two, he felt someone's eyes on him. But he didn't pay much attention. However, when Rama emerged from her flat, he had no choice but to look at her.

'Namaste ji,' she responded with a smile to Ali Amjad's salaam. She was inordinately proud of her smile. 'You are Ali Amjadji, isn't it?'

'Yes.' What else could he do but answer, even though he had already unlocked the door.

'How much rent are you paying?'

'Six hundred and fifty.'

'Hey Ram! God save us from these Sindhis. You should be paying standard rent. I'm Mrs Rama Chopra. And bhai sahib, now that you've come to live here, stay away from Mrs Gupta. The moment she gets a chance she'll borrow twenty-thirty rupees and nick something from your home, all in the blink of an eye. She's really quick with her hands...' In her eagerness, she forgot that she had come out of her flat pretending she was in a big hurry. She began giving a running commentary on Sursingar – 'This Frenny, who lives in number four, is not worth meeting. I don't want to say anything but ... You'll find out yourself...'

Soon it was clear that apart from the Chopras, there was nobody worth knowing in Sursingar.

'When will bhabhiji arrive?'

'The day after.' His sister-in-law was coming from Benares, especially to see a film shoot and to meet Dilip Kumar.

'Then bhabhiji and I will go and see a matinee show every day.' Rama laughed heartily and then said, 'Nath has no interests whatsoever. He just comes back from work and sits down with his whisky. But he has a good heart.'

Ali Amjad opened the door of his house. But Rama didn't take the hint. She prattled on, 'Just that no one should touch his phone – that's all. The thing is, bhai sahib, there is only one phone in the building. Ours. Now if we start delivering messages to everyone in the building, we won't have time for anything else. I used to be great friends with Mrs Chintak, who lives in number six. Mr Chintak works in some daily paper. So this one time, Mrs Chintak went to her mother's place. Bhai sahib, for four months I fed Mr Chintak at my home. I would pay the dhobi for his laundry. Now I'm not the sort to keep account, bhai sahib, but feeding a man for four months costs money, doesn't it? One day, there was a phone call for him. I was having a bath, the servant had gone to the market. Nath was shaving. So, he said there was no one to deliver a message at that moment. That was it, bhai sahib, what should I say? When Mrs Chintak returned, she created such a big fuss around this little incident. Nath too is a bit quick with his tongue. He got annoyed. He said, "Will you get out of my house or should I hit you with my shoe?" She fled the flat in fear, but once she was outside she began talking rubbish about my Mita, saying – god forbid – that she had something going with a Muslim boy. Don't mind, bhai sahib, but neither Mita nor I like Muslims … Oh dear. I've gone quite mad, telling *you* that I don't like Muslims…'

Ali Amjad extricated himself with great difficulty, and entered his flat. And Rama went back to hers. The telephone in the sitting room was locked. Bholanath thought that he was the only one with a key to it. The thing is, Rama loved chatting on the phone and Bholanath was the one who had to pay the bills. But Rama was cunning. She bought another, similar lock. She kept one key for herself and sold the old lock and key to Mrs Midha, who had just acquired a new phone for her bedroom. Rama scared her by telling her that her neighbours would use her phone so often, the bill would be bigger than her grocery bill. That's why a lock was necessary. Sarla was in Rama's house when this conversation took place. Sarla Midha swallowed this story and said that she'd pick up a lock on her way home. So Rama passed off her phone lock with its one key to her. When Sarla asked about a second key, Rama told her that phone locks came with just one key. And so, without spending any money of her own, she got her own key to the phone and would keep dialling Delhi to talk to Mita, since Mita had moved there with her husband by then. And when a huge phone bill would arrive, Bholanath would shout and scream and bring the house down, while she would sit merrily munching on apples or grapefruit. This would irritate Bholanath even more, and then Rama would stop eating, sharpen her claws, and go after him, pointing out that the phone was always locked ... To which Bholanath had no answer...

... As soon as she returned to her flat after meeting Ali Amjad, she went and folded her hands in front of the idol of Krishna, then took the key out from under it and unlocked the phone to talk to Sarla. She kept the key hidden there because Bholanath was an atheist and never went anywhere near the idol. He ate beef too, and Rama had secretly kept aside separate utensils for him. The money she nicked from Bholanath's wallet was also kept hidden under Krishna. And every other day, some servant or the other would be kicked out for stealing this money...

... So, she took the key out from under the statue and phoned Mrs Midha. 'Sarla, I have something really interesting to tell you...' And she told her all about her meeting with Ali Amjad. Sarla kept asking her if she had *really* told him she didn't like socializing with Muslims. And each time Rama replied that did Sarla think she was too scared to say such a thing?

Sarla Midha was one of those women who, even in their wildest dreams, would never think of carrying on with a Muslim woman. Forget Muslims, she didn't even eat food that had been touched by Midha sahib. She had her own food cooked separately ... And now she was afraid that Ali Amjad and his family would start visiting Rama. Also, though Rama had not yet responded to any of the hints she had dropped, Sarla hadn't given up hope ... Sarla's tragedy was that she was an artist and she couldn't just report her feelings in the way newspapers reported the news. She enjoyed the chase more than actually getting what she wanted. That's why she wanted to keep Rama away from Muslims. And Rama's tragedy was that she liked the good things in life, and Bholanath's income was not enough to support the lifestyle she wanted. So she didn't want to let go of Sarla, because it was Sarla who paid for her fondness for watching films, who gifted her new and expensive saris on her birthday, made her wear them, and then, in front of everyone, hugged and kissed her...

Meaning, both Rama and Sarla needed each other.

But Rama was also a bit envious of Sarla, and this envy wasn't entirely unnatural either. Sarla had money but no interests. Rama had interests but no money. To fulfil her smallest fancies, she had to nick money from Bholanath and then get an honest servant kicked out on the charge of stealing.

But Rama knew how to hide her envy and loathing. That's why she lost no time in making friends with Seema. For a couple of days after Seema's arrival, she tried to lure her into making friendly overtures with fake smiles and 'hello jis'. She wanted Seema to make the first move so that she could tell everyone that *she* hadn't wanted to engage with Seema at all, but what could you do if the other person wouldn't take no for an answer? You would have to meet the person, wouldn't you?

But Seema had already been warned by Ali Amjad: 'Bhabhi, it'll be something of a feat if you manage to escape Mrs Khatak. She's not a woman, she's a leech, a leech. Once she sticks to you, it's impossible to shake her off.'

Seema had come from Govindpura Kalan in Benares to watch film shoots, shop a little and get herself photographed with film stars. Where was the time for

Mrs Khatak? She had begun asking Ali Amjad questions about which film star was shooting where and who he was friends with the moment she got off at Bombay Central station.

But Rama was not one to admit defeat so easily. At first, she kept waiting for Seema to visit. But when Seema maintained her distance, she got fed up, arrived at number two Sursingar with Khatakji in tow, and rang the bell.

'Tell your sahib that we have come,' Rama said.

'Sahib isn't home,' the servant replied.

'Call your memsahib then.'

'Memsahib isn't home either.'

'Oh. But come, let's at least have a look at the house,' Rama said, and walked into the flat. Bholanath followed her. The poor servant had no way of stopping them. But he followed them around as Rama inspected the entire flat. She wasn't impressed. There was nothing in bright, gaudy colours anywhere. Just plenty of vases full of fresh flowers. On the sitting-room wall hung a Picasso print. *Seated Female Nude*.

Rama strained her eyes trying to spot the nude woman but failed. In the bedroom, she couldn't get past the olive velvet bedspread ... She decided there and then that she too would get a velvet bedspread, throw out the plastic flowers from her vases and hang a painting on the wall. She bought a painting that very day. Framed watercolours and oil paintings of landscapes were sold in front of Haji Ali, near the racecourse. She had gone there with Mrs Midha. The ostensible reason was that they were going to Metro for a matinee show. As they were passing by the National Sports Club, she stopped the car with a 'Hai!' as soon as she spotted the landscapes.

'This will look lovely in your bedroom. And this in the drawing room...' She began choosing paintings for Sarla. She picked out a painting of an aged cow grazing in the fields, then left it, saying there would be no place in Sarla's house for it. So Sarla bought it for her.

When Khatakji came home that night, he saw the painting hanging on the bedroom wall. Rama promptly began telling him a story about an artist who had come to their door to sell his art. He was asking for sixty. She convinced him to part with it for ten. Bholanath happened to be in a good mood, so nothing further was said, and Rama even managed to extract ten rupees from him.

The next day, when Seema was buying flowers from the flower-seller at her door, Rama came out of her flat.

'Namaste. Pansy...'

'Namaste.'

Rama too sat down next to the flower-seller's basket.

'We came to see you yesterday.'

'Yes. We had gone for a film muhurat.'

'Who is working in the film?'

'Dharmendra and Hema Malini. How much for the carnations?' Seema started talking to the flower-seller. 'You really charge too much...'

'No, bai. I come to this building only because of you. If you say I charge too much, how will I make a living?'

'I'm fond of flowers too. But flower-sellers don't come here. How much for the tube roses?'

Rama was compelled to buy the flowers, because she had to prove to Seema that she too was very fond of flowers. Seema bought flowers worth thirty-five rupees. Rama chose flowers worth forty-five and then went inside, saying she had to get the money. But she kept lurking at the door, waiting for Seema to go back to her flat. Seema paid the flower-seller, picked up the flowers and went in. When the door shut behind her, Rama emerged and asked the flower-seller, 'Do you have change for a thousand?' Obviously he didn't. So he said, 'Never mind, bai, I'll take the money tomorrow.' But

Rama wasn't going to get trapped. She said, 'I don't believe in credit...' And with that she shut the door and latched it from inside.

Rama was delighted to have proved to Seema that she wasn't the only one in the building who bought flowers. But she was still bothered by the fact that Seema had not brought up the matter of invitations to muhurats. The entire project of becoming friendly, of meeting, had to be put off again.

That night she told Bholanath, 'Mr Amjad's sister-in-law seems very proud.'

Bholanath was tired and the conversation ended there.

A few more days passed. The two women only bumped into each other when the flower and vegetable-sellers arrived with their baskets. And the conversation would end once the flower and vegetable-sellers left with their baskets. Seema didn't go anywhere, nor did anyone come to visit her.

Finally, Mrs Gupta couldn't contain herself and, one day, she rang the bell and went in. Shrikant Gupta stayed in number ten. He was the secretary of Sursingar Cooperative Housing Society Private Limited and also a homeopathic doctor. He lived in Bandra and practised in Borivali. He was a writer too, and Mrs Gupta's husband.

All three were full-time jobs, but Guptaji did them in such a way that none of the three knew about the other. His practice wasn't going well. His writing wasn't going well. Being a husband wasn't going well either. He did the bare minimum of anything that was required. In Sursingar, he was known as Mrs Gupta's husband. He never socialized with anyone. He would leave early in the morning, come back late at night, eat his dinner, go to sleep. Seema only saw him for the first time about two months after coming to Sursingar.

But Mrs Gupta was totally different. She shared everyone's joys and sorrows, and made sure everyone shared hers. Nobody knew her name. She was known only as Mrs Gupta. The grown-ups called her Mrs Gupta and the younger ones Gupta aunty. She must have had a name, of course. But she used it only once every five years, when she went to cast her vote.

... Mrs Gupta was sociable, so she couldn't cope with the 'curfew' imposed by Rama. She was also hamstrung by her own weaknesses and helplessness. So, hiding from Rama, she landed up at Seema's place.

Seema was feeding her daughter milk, while her son Waseem was racing his battery-operated car on the carpet and masterminding accidents. He would pretend to be the driver of the cars involved in the accidents, then turn into a policeman writing out a challan or taking a bribe.

Mrs Gupta brushed her hand over Waseem's head affectionately. He took no notice because he was busy playing the role of a policeman accepting a bribe.

'Rascal,' Seema scolded him. 'You didn't do adaab to aunty.'

Waseem swung around and did an adaab.

Mrs Gupta started laughing. 'Arre, let it be behenji, children are like this nowadays.' Fatima had wet her nappy. Mrs Gupta immediately moved to help. While changing the nappy, she said, 'This Bholanath is a real bastard...' Seema gave her no encouragement. Not that Mrs Gupta needed any. She kept talking, 'I don't meddle into anyone's affairs, behenji. But what can I say? This building is not worth staying in. Patel is a eunuch. Fenny gets by with paying guests. Bholanath has a roving eye. Mrs Chintak and Rama didn't fight over the phone. It was because Bholanath tried to make advances towards Mrs Chintak. And when she didn't rise to the bait, he told Rama that she was making advances towards him.' Mrs Gupta laughed. 'Only a madwoman would try and flirt with Bholanath. But Rama and

Bholanath are a strange couple. She believes that every woman is out to get him, and he believes that every man is out to get her. The two of them had a fight with Manchandani and Sadhna over this very thing. Before that, the four of them used to be such good friends! Neither couple could bear to be away from the other. Manchandani would call Rama "Rama behen", and Bholanath would call Sadhna "bhabhiji". Manchandani didn't have a phone then. Bholanath wanted to invest some money with Manchandani, because how long could the friendship with Mrs Midha last? Mrs Midha is a little different, if you know what I mean, and Rama may have a thousand faults, but not *that*. But what was I saying? Yes, Manchandani didn't have a phone. Then he got a phone, but didn't get into any kind of partnership with Bholanath, and that's when Bholanath decided that Manchandani had designs on Rama. Husband and wife fought bitterly. Bholanath got a heart attack. Rama said she would commit suicide. But then both of them abandoned the idea of killing themselves, and it was decided that Rama would tie a rakhi on Manchandani.' Saying this, Mrs Gupta laughed and continued, 'Rama's rakhi was proof that Bholanath once again suspected her…'

But Seema went back home after telling him these stories, and Ali Amjad was left alone in this woefully out-of-tune Sursingar Housing Society. Every single person in the society spent three-quarters of their spare time checking on their neighbours.

While Seema was there, she'd held the fort. She loved collecting scandals. Which was why she could tolerate Rama, Mrs Gupta and the other 'ladies'. But she enjoyed gossiping the most with Nazma.

Nazma was a call girl.

In Benares, Seema could never have dreamt of meeting a call girl so openly. Rama and Mrs Gupta had provided several crucial facts about Nazma:

1. That Nazma was not a day younger than thirty-two, though she claimed she was twenty-four.
2. That Nazma was not as beautiful as she appeared.
3. That she charged four to five hundred rupees per night.
4. That she gave the men of Sursingar a concession.
5. That she was supported by some rich man who paid her rent and bought all her imported make-up.
6. That she supported Harish Rai.

7. That Nazma, going by the name of Neeli, used to do small roles in films and was very popular among assistant directors.
8. That she knew, and had a soft spot for, Harish from those film days.
9. That because she was friendly with Ali Amjad, Harish had given him a film to write. Otherwise, why would Harish leave Ramnath, who had written silver jubilee films for him?

Seema was an outspoken girl. She asked Harish outright.

'Bhabhi,' said Harish, 'what is true, what is false, nobody knows...' The truth was that this was a line from Harish's previous film. A hit line of dialogue written by Ramnath. Harish liked Ramnath's lines because, despite mistakes of spelling and grammar, they could be used in any situation.

But Seema was a simple, straightforward girl. She spoke normally, simply. She neither spoke nor understood filmy dialogues. She cut Harish down to size by saying, 'What you just said was a lie, and the truth is what you will tell me now.'

Harish was stumped. He began laughing.

He was not seriously in love with Nazma. He had met her on a film set and had taken a liking to her. At that time, he used to stay in Andheri East. A one-bedroom-hall flat. And he was alone. Ali Amjad, VD and Alimullah lived in D'Cruz Guest House.

VD and Rosy's one-sided love affair continued, though Rosy no longer stayed in Mai's Adda. She was in Colaba. She had started a business there. But that had no effect on VD's love. He went to meet Rosy at least a couple of times every week. He never complained. They would have simple conversations.

'How are you?'

'I'm all right. How are you?'

'I'm fine too.'

'Will you have some tea?'

This little conversation would take an hour, or an hour and a half.

One day, VD was very sad. He told Alimullah, 'Yaar, it's the same scene all the time. It feels like a film shoot that's going on and on, where both of us are giving retake after retake. But the shot is never okayed.'

Alimullah kept quiet because he didn't understand film analogies. He said, 'Yaar, VD, I can't understand why you don't get out of that sister-fucker prostitute's clutches.'

'You just used a masculine adjective for a woman.' VD was fond of pointing out mistakes in Alimullah's grammar. 'Listen to these lines by Rahi Masoom Raza. The scene goes like this. The heroine, who is a streetwalker, gives a local gangster called Raja her earnings because she's under the impression that he's like Tarzan, the Dadar gangster. But Raja is the hero. How can he be like that? He slaps Ganga. Ganga is the heroine's name. The side hero is Himmat Jaunpuri. He tells Raja that he shouldn't hit a woman. To which Raja says, "You call a bloody whore a woman?" That's it. The side hero gets the chance to make a speech: "At least she doesn't sell counterfeit boot polish like you do. At least she doesn't adulterate milk with water or rice with stones. At least she doesn't sell fake medicine, fake booze, fake dreams and fake futures. She just sells her body – without adulteration, without playing a role, without giving lectures. She sells her honour, yes, but there's nothing dishonourable about her."' VD stopped.

There was silence in the room. A heavy, soiled, rancid silence.

'The bloody public will applaud this speech,' VD said after a while, and lit his Charminar. Alimullah said nothing. He knew that VD periodically suffered from bouts of bitterness.

'What has happened to the bloody writer of *Aadha Gaon*?' VD asked.

'I haven't read *Aadha Gaon*,' Alimullah said. 'I don't know Hindi.'

'Everything is fucked,' VD said.

'I got another letter from Amma today,' Alimullah said.

'I can tell you what it says without even looking,' VD said. 'Yaar, why are mothers' letters so monotonous? Everything is all right here. Just hearing this sets my hair down there on fire.'

'The meaning of "all right" has changed.' Harish walked in. He was with Nazma. 'We are all right means we haven't died yet, we're still alive.'

Nazma burst out laughing.

'The people in our country, they've become used to sorrow. Virendra Kumar, aka VD, there is a lot of sorrow here.'

'Wrong,' VD said. 'If there was too much sorrow, it would have been taxed by now.'

Nazma felt like laughing again, but she stopped herself when she saw VD's grave expression. Harish pulled out a tin of 555s. A tin of 555s was a status symbol in the film world. Harish had already turned director. He could not smoke Wills Flake or Charminar. He even had a gold lighter. 22 carat gold.

VD lit his cigarette with a match. He had a theory that half the enjoyment of a cigarette was lost if you used a lighter.

'This is my film's heroine, Nazma,' Harish introduced her.

'Real name Halima, fake name Nazma, screen name Neeli,' Nazma said.

'Why Neeli?' VD asked. 'You're dusky, not blue.'

VD was utterly serious. But Nazma and everyone else laughed as if he'd cracked a joke, and the bitterness in the room tiptoed out, to lose itself among the crowds of Veer Savarkar Marg, aka Porbandar Road, or to jump into Bandra Talao.

'Alimullah got another letter from his mother today,' VD said.

But Nazma had no interest in Alimullah, his mother or VD. She wasn't particularly pleased about coming to D'Cruz either. She was a film's heroine, a financier's mistress and a director's lover. She had her own Italian Fiat car. There was nothing in common between Nazma and D'Cruz. But Harish had insisted she come. Managing her French chiffon sari, protecting it actually, she sat there with great difficulty, counting the cigarette butts that lay scattered on the floor. She had counted forty-three when she sensed someone calling her.

'Nazma, take a look at Alimullah's fiancée.' Harish extended a small photograph towards her. She took it from him and looked. The girl had tried very hard to be fashionable. Her eyes had been made up like Hema Malini's. Her smile was in the Meena Kumari style. The slant of her neck was like Waheeda Rehman's. She had Sharmila Tagore-like dimples in her cheeks...

'She's not a girl, she's a box of assorted sweets,' VD quipped and Nazma laughed again. That sparkler of a laugh. Alimullah did not like it. VD's case was different. He was a friend. He could say anything. But this woman, who was spread out like a bed-sheet, could not laugh at the woman that Alimullah's mother had chosen to be his wife.

That was it. Matters got out of hand. VD took Nazma's side. And why would he not? He was a born proletariat. Agitated, he sat up straight on the bed as usual, and taking deep drags of his cigarette, coughing all the while, he launched into a speech.

'What do you think of yourself?' he said, using the formal Hindi word for 'you'.

When VD was angry, he'd become extra polite.

To cut a long story short, the incident ended with Alimullah deciding that he would leave D'Cruz that very night. Harish tried to reason with him. Ali Amjad, who had landed up in the middle of the fight, also tried to talk to him. But Alimullah was adamant.

And so, Ali Amjad and VD were left alone in D'Cruz, with five months of unpaid rent and their lonely lives. That night passed with great difficulty in room number five of D'Cruz Guest House.

VD knew how to laugh at his life's desolation, which was why, perhaps, he was thought of as a jovial person. But Ali Amjad did not know the art of hiding his sorrow.

It was a very strange night. The silence in the room was so rough and full of grit, it scraped away at the soft covers of thought. VD was on the bed. Ali Amjad was on the sofa ... And VD was sad.

Suddenly, he said, 'Yaar, I don't know how to be sad. I find it very boring.'

'Why did you have to make fun of Alimullah's fiancée?'

'When I laugh at myself, Alimullah never feels bad. Saeeda is a brand-new fiancée, yaar! I'm his childhood friend. We both failed class nine together. We fell in love for the first time together…'

The room was silent again because Ali Amjad didn't ask any questions about that first love. Their heads resting on hard, dirty pillows, they stared at the ceiling and smoked their cigarettes.

After a while, VD said, 'You won't ask me anything about that first love?'

'No,' Ali Amjad said.

He had his own incomplete loves. Ruqaiya, Sabiha, Kishwar … And what was her name? Yes, Lata. It felt as if these names had come out of stories from previous lifetimes. Or as if these names belonged to someone else's life or story. As if he was just a spectator … Sitting far away, watching the spectacle of his own life. When you see your scars, you remember the wounds, but you don't remember the pain from those wounds, do you?

What is memory?
The scar from a wound,
Or a familiar path.
Footprints of pain obscuring the footprints of
dreams.

Slowly, slowly
The footprints of dreams and
The footprints of pain
Go into the wasteland of time
With the wild heron
And fall, tired perhaps –
And fall, dying perhaps
Who will go into the wasteland
of time for them!

Ruqaiya, Sabiha, Kishwar and Lata Sinha ... Four names. Four ordinary-sounding names. God knows how many Ruqaiyas, Sabhias, Kishwars and Lata Sinhas there would be in India and Pakistan.

But why Pakistan?

But why not Pakistan? Ruqaiya was in Pakistan. Sabiha was in Pakistan. Kishwar was in Pakistan. Lata Sinha was in Pakistan. Whatever's been left behind is in Pakistan. Estrangement has many names now. There are many kinds of estrangement too, now. Estrangement that's within the house. Estrangement that's outside the house. Estrangement that's home-grown. Estrangement that's foreign ... There used to be that 'Rattumal Bhonduprasad'. Yes, Babu Triloknath Srivastava.

Slightly repressed. With a straggly pigtail. A grimy dhoti. A bright kurta. Apparently, he had gone to New York and become T.P. Srivastava. The remaining letters of his name and his pigtail had vanished. A couple of years ago, he had come to visit India on a tourist visa. His fair-skinned wife, Mrs Sara Srivastava, had come with him ... TP had become American. And he was as excited as his wife to see India...

TP.

An imported estrangement. The estrangement of speaking Hindi with an English accent. The estrangement of mispronouncing 'daal'...

Ruqaiya, Sabiha, Kishwar and Lata Sinha. Estrangement that was stuck like a postage stamp on an envelope. I've reached Pakistan safely. I think of you a lot. I don't like anything because you aren't here. The day it gets too much, I'll leave everything and run away to be with you. If you aren't with me, I can't even stay in god's heaven, let alone Pakistan ... Ali Amjad remembered this letter from god's own land[2] by heart. He couldn't remember whether this letter had been

[2] *God's Own Land* is the name of a novel by the Pakistani novelist, Shaukat Siddiqui.

written by Ruqaiya or Sabiha. Their letters were very similar ... Then both got married. Ali Amjad found out that both were very happy. Their husbands were also very happy. The only person who wasn't happy was Ali Amjad. But he was very far away from them.

And what about the two years and twelve days between Ruqaiya and Sabiha? How did those two years and twelve days pass? And had they really passed? He trembled at the question.

'Say what you want. But Alimullah shouldn't have done this,' Ali Amjad said.

'But I'm not saying anything,' VD said.

Once again, there was silence in the room.

After some time, VD himself said, 'The thing is, Alimullah has his own problems. He's been wanting to leave for quite a few months. But he didn't know how to say it. He's going to get married. His responsibilities will increase. Today I felt sorry for him, so I gave him the opportunity to get angry.'

'So what will you do now?' Ali Amjad asked heartlessly.

'I'll make friends with someone else,' VD said simply. 'Actually, I've thought of a business.'

'Business? And you?' Ali Amjad sat up.

'Yes.' VD lit one cigarette with another. 'I'm going to start selling myself. No sales tax on that.'

VD laughed loudly at his own remark. In the silence of that Bombay night, his laughter was frightful. Ali Amjad recoiled. He looked out of the window. On the broken steps of the pond on Ghorbandar Road a woman squatted, washing her face, and a bhaiyya from north India rushed by, his bicycle laden with cans of milk...

The very next day, Alimullah came to make up with VD. But VD said all sorts of things to him and threw him out of the room. Ali Amjad was there, he knew everything, but could say nothing.

After that, VD and Alimullah stopped talking to each other. Alimullah didn't even invite him to his wedding. Quietly, he left the world of D'Cruz, and maybe he even forgot D'Cruz altogether. He got a one-bedroom-hall flat for himself in Jogeshwari. He had his own wife. His own scooter. What else does one need to live?

Alimullah's wife, Saeeda, tried very hard to get VD to visit their Jogeshwari flat. But VD stayed unmoved. He made three new friends. He was also happy that his new business had taken off.

He thought life was all about running a workshop

for beggars, pining for Rosy, drinking country liquor at Mai's Adda, and eating fried fish ... Perhaps.

Rosy was alone in Cuffe Parade.

Alimullah was alone in the one-bedroom-hall Jogeshwari flat, and Saeeda, lying in bed next to him, was also alone because Alimullah was like medicine – only to be had before meals!

Harish was alone in a three-bedroom-hall flat in Juhu-Parle Scheme. He had two cars and kept three women. And he in turn was kept by Nazma. And he was alone ... Because the flat in which he lived as if he owned it had Nazma's name on it. Harish was alone because, like Alimullah and Ali Amjad, he had also taken 'sick leave' from Marxism. The day he started drinking Royal Salute, he stopped meeting VD.

Ali Amjad didn't like it. But VD laughed this off too.

'Arre yaar, who has the time to think of all these things?' he said, lighting a Charminar. 'The person who doesn't meet us is not our Harish. Our Harish could think and live in this grubby room. This Harish needs a suite in Sun-n-Sand to think. A Mont Blanc pen to write. Royal Salute whisky to drink. A Dunlopillo mattress to sleep on. And top-class girls to sleep with. Screw Harish. I want a dialogue writer.'

'What do you want?' Ali Amjad asked in surprise.

'Dialogue writer,' VD said. 'Will you work with me?'

'Arre, but why do you need a dialogue writer?'

'How can I manage with just one dialogue writer?' VD said. 'Today I have three dialogue writers, two directors, fifteen make-up men and four dress designers working for me. I want to put you in charge of the writing department.'

For the first time, Ali Amjad looked at VD carefully. His clothes were nice, clean. The lighter with which he'd lit his Charminar was made of gold. His spectacle frames were mother of pearl. He wore a platinum signet ring on the middle finger of his right hand...

VD smiled. He said, 'I've started a business of second-hand life.'

'Are you making a film?'

'Am I an imbecile that I'll make a film? I'm running a workshop for beggars.'

Ali Amjad couldn't believe what he was hearing.

'I'll give you two thousand rupees a month,' VD said. 'Think about it.'

What was there to think about? Ali Amjad had been unemployed for four months. But...

Naturally, there would be a 'but' here.

'The thing is, educated people have never thought about begging. Until now, this racket was in the hands of goons and, as you know, goons have no aesthetic sense. Pop somebody's eye out and make him a blind beggar. Break somebody else's legs ... etc., etc. One day, when I was just lying around, I had this brainwave that if one were to scientifically organize beggars, one could earn a lot of money...'

It turned out that VD had indeed given the matter a great deal of thought. It was a dangerous business. After all, why would the people who ran begging rackets in big cities allow some Virendra Kumar, MA (Economics), to push his way into their business? But VD was a stubborn man. He dug his heels in – this is what he would do.

So one day, he went to Haji Fakira saying he had a plan that would suit his line of work. Haji Fakira also happened to be on the lookout for something to invest his money in.

No one in Bombay knew that Haji Fakira's real name was Shivmangal Prasad. After committing three murders in Pilibhit, he'd fled to Bombay and become Haji Fakira. He grew a beard. His forehead bore the imprint of his prostrations before Allah. He even had a minor operation so that there would be no question of any suspicion. In a few years, he became a well-known Muslim League leader from the Bhendi Bazaar-Mohammad Ali Road-JJ Hospital area. When the corporation elections were held, he contested on a League ticket and won. But his real business was selling foreign money in black to hajis and getting them to bring back foreign goods. Gradually, as his work took off, he took on a film starlet as his mistress and went on hajj. His influence in the police department grew by the day. Leaders from Akhil Bhartiya Pidhi began going to his house for tea and to collect funds for their party ... He gained more and more respect in society. He was elected president of many school committees. Once he got elected president, he had to learn how to sign, and that's how VD met him for the first time. He took a great liking to VD, and so VD became his secretary. He wrote speeches for him. And he also taught him a few dozen English words to sprinkle his conversations with, so that he would come across as an educated person. In the Bombay Corporation elections, people voted generously for Haji sahib's candidates because they knew that he was their man. He was friends with ministers. He got along with members of the opposition too. The police took their salaries from the government but listened to him…

Since VD was the reason why Haji sahib began to be counted among the well-educated, he earned the respect of Haji sahib's posse as well. People tried to ingratiate themselves with VD so that he would put in a good word and get their work done. He too became envied and feared … And slowly, Haji sahib came to depend more and more on him.

Lakhs of rupees passed through VD's hands, but despite Haji sahib's insistence he didn't leave room number five in D'Cruz for the Sursingar flat Haji sahib had bought just for him.

The thing is, VD believed in doing favours but was against taking them. Many a time, he had stomped off after an argument to sulk at home (i.e., number five, D'Cruz) until finally Haji sahib had to send someone to call him back. The idea of opening a workshop for beggars also came to him just like that one day. Haji sahib was annoyed about something, and he had responded haughtily: 'I'm your employee, not a lackey. Keep your job. I'm going to D'Cruz.'

Haji sahib was a very practical man. He had asked, 'Will you commit suicide, or beg on the streets?'

At that moment, he didn't know how to answer the question. He went to Mai's Adda and drank quietly until, all of a sudden, he came up with a scheme – to open a training centre for beggars. He thought of a name in English – The Beggars Workshop Pvt. Ltd. It would have to be Pvt. Ltd. because he knew that, once it took off, the competition would be tough, and the truth was, he thought of Haji sahib only because of his fear of the competition.

'Wonderful,' Haji sahib said with a laugh when he saw him. 'You're reforming. You came back without needing to be cajoled.'

'I figured out a new business, so I thought I'd ask you first,' VD said. 'If you refuse, I'll go talk to someone else...'

But why would Haji Fakira refuse?

And so the Beggars Workshop started. It was decided to form an All-India Beggars Union. This union would work to unite and organize all beggars.

VD had spent a lot of time and effort thinking about this issue. He believed that if beggars continued begging in the same area, people would soon get used to them, the way they got used to signboards for shops or electric poles. The result: a drop in income. That's why he decided that not only should beggars change locations, they should also change cities. Just like government officers got transferred, beggars also needed to be transferred. Those who were loyal to the union would get good centres: Bombay, Calcutta, Delhi, Benares, Allahabad, Ajmer ... And those who were troublesome would be sent to Ghazipur, Pratapgarh and other such awful places, like punishment postings...

The people of India love to beg and to give beggars money. The ones who can't give money begin to beg for it in one way or another. Meaning, all social life is strung together on a thread of begging and, therefore, if one could use begging for political purposes, the Beggars Union could capture the Indian republic...

VD cast such a spell with his talk that Haji Fakira began dreaming of becoming the president of India. And that's how VD became the be-all and end-all of the Beggars Workshop. And even VD's enemies had to concede that he slogged his butt off for it.

The workshop was started in an old garage in Jogeshwari to begin with. It was a two-storey building. Two garages on the ground floor. And on top, three rooms, a small balcony and a toilet-cum-bathroom.

One of the garages was converted into an office. The second one had a costume section, a make-up room and properties. Classes were held in the three upstairs rooms.

VD wanted to turn begging into a commercial art. That's why he wanted to employ some dialogue writers, some make-up people and a couple of directors who would teach the beggars how to beg properly. In the beginning, other beggars paid no attention to the Beggars Workshop. But when they started facing competition from the workshop beggars, they realized that they were no match. Therefore, enrolments in the workshop slowly grew, and VD acquired a car and two bodyguards. Because it wasn't easy for those running the begging racket to countenance its existence, the workshop was attacked a couple of times. VD was threatened too. And here's where Haji Fakira was of particular help. A beggars' army was set up and Haji Fakira became its leader. This is what he said at a press conference:

'Our society and government may like it or not, but the fact remains that in our country 1 to 1.25 crore people work as beggars on a permanent basis, and 3 to 3.5 crore on a temporary basis. Meaning, after Muslims, beggars are India's largest minority and, like Muslims and Harijans, they too have every right to live and conduct their business here ... And I have decided to fight their battle for them. Today, I want to announce that all those who speak out against the beggars' army will have their mouths smashed in...'

And when some opponents literally had their mouths smashed in, those who ran their own begging rackets realized that to fight against the workshop was to invite trouble ... So, the workshop soon had a monopoly over begging in the city of Bombay.

... Ali Amjad was flabbergasted. He looked at VD who was smiling like some divine being.

'What's the harm in trying?' VD said. 'Two thousand rupees a month is not a small amount. Think about it.'

'I'll try it,' Ali Amjad said.

'Then I'll book a room at the Taj tomorrow. Sit with Harish and work on a script.'

'With Harish!'

'Officially, it's his fourth assistant who works at the workshop,' VD said. 'But since you'll write the dialogues, there's no need to hide anything from you.'

So it was fixed.

The next day, Harish and Ali Amjad met at the Taj. Neither was prepared to speak the truth. It was agreed that both of them were doing VD a favour. It was an old friendship. Neither had thought that VD could sink to such depths.

Only when they had said all this to each other, drunk 'gin and ginger', made forty-fifty phone calls to writers, producers and directors, telling them that they were calling from the Taj where they were writing a script, did they get down to work.

Harish and Ali Amjad had just about fixed a name for the hero, that is, the beggar, when VD showed up.

'I've just got news that there have been serious Hindu–Muslim riots in Shahjahanpur. Leave that Bihar script alone. People are bored of stories of famine and starvation anyway. Arre, if so many people in Bombay are dying of hunger, who cares about Bihar's hungry? Are they special? I've also heard that the film-wallahs are going to march for the Biharis. Who will look at our artists when they have Dilip Kumar, Raj Kapoor, Dev Anand, Rajesh Khanna and Dharmendra? So while the film-wallahs ask for charity for the Biharis, why not cash in on the Shahjahanpur riots? Prepare two scripts. One for Bhendi Bazaar and one for Shivaji Park...'

'All right.'

'A hundred people from each side will come from

Shahjahanpur by the day after,' VD said. 'We've asked for a few women and children too.'

Ali Amjad had a spectacular idea.

'Yaar, get a few young girls as well. Rape will make for a good story.'

'Rape?' Harish was startled. 'No, bhai. Who's going to sympathize with the rape of beggar women?'

'Not beggars. Hindu and Muslim girls,' VD said.

Silence descended upon the room.

Perhaps all three of them were ashamed of themselves. Perhaps none of them realized how far they had sunk. Perhaps none of them could even recognize themselves.

The word Shahjahanpur had become indecent, like abuse directed towards mothers and sisters.

'Yaar, VD...' Harish began to say something, then stopped.

'This is not the age of protest,' VD said. 'Bow your head and learn to accept reality.' Silence again. 'Or commit suicide. You, Ali Amjad, are not a character in a novel that you must keep fighting. You are you. I am I. Ali Amjad is Ali Amjad. All of us think something but do something else. In this contradiction, lies our life's truth, its reality.'

No one said anything.

Ali Amjad took out a fresh sheet of paper to write the second script on.

VD stood up.

'I'll be off then. I have to fix the Filmfare awards.'

'What do you have to do with the awards?' Ali Amjad asked enviously.

VD smiled.

'The All-India Beggars Union has 9,80,712 members. If I won't have anything to do with the awards, who will? I have a monopoly in sending song requests to Akashvani and Radio Ceylon. I can turn any music director you want into a flop. Recently, I had carried out an agitation against the film *Raen Basera* because it had a thief who was named Valmiki ... You think I'm related to Valmiki? But big producers and directors are against Chhediram Gavara because he started this trend of low-budget films and important people are praising his work. There's an Anti-Chhediram Gavara Fund as well, whose job is to make his films flop. I'm a permanent invitee to the working committee of the Anti-Chhediram Gavara Fund. Arre ... I forgot to mention another important thing. I need dialogues for a campaign. I have to create buzz about Rajesh Khanna being a better actor than Dilip Kumar.'

'But who will believe it, yaar?' Ali Amjad said.

'Nobody,' VD said. 'We also have to spread the rumour that Rajesh Khanna is spending money to get a Filmfare award. He's probably doing that anyway. But the Beggars Union is going to ensure that this year's award goes to Manoj Kumar. There's a meeting for that in half an hour...'

VD left.

Harish lay down.

'Yaar, what is this fucking nonsense we've got ourselves into?' Ali Amjad asked.

For a while Harish looked at him through half-closed eyes as if he was contemplating an answer. Then he said:

'We'll call the Hindu girl Lata.'

'Eh?'

'The question is, should she be Lata Mathur or Lata Gupta?'

'Where did this Hindu girl come from, yaar?'

'From Shahjahanpur,' said Harish. 'Lata Sinha sounds nice.'

Ruqaiya, Sabiha, Kishwar and Lata Sinha.

Before my eyes
The tired sun of the day

Gets lost in the evening's foliage.
And I
Afflicted by the pain of separation
A stranger to my own shadow,
Am left standing alone on the road...

Ali Amjad lay down as well. He was exhausted from remembering Ruqaiya, Sabiha, Kishwar and Lata Sinha. Memory is not something light, like a cluster of clouds, that it can just pass by without your feeling it. Each and every memory is a life gone by ... And no life is lightweight.

Ali Amjad looked at his reflection in the dressing-table mirror. He couldn't recognize himself. He had changed so much. He shut his eyes and began humming:

The worlds I am estranged from, how are they
now
How are the blossoming branches
The houses made of flowers
The lane that taught me what love is
Does it remember my footprints?
What winds blow in the city of my humiliation
How does it treat its lovers

What is the value to perishing in love
The moon must still appear
But to whom does the moonlight
Tell its stories of love
The moon must be sleepless
I was like a stone,
Thrown away
It was the right thing to do
But the glass houses in that city, how do they fare…

'Yaar, till one doesn't decide how old she is, what she looks like, how can one think about her?' Harish's voice seemed to be coming from very far away.

'Whose looks?' Ali Amjad asked, startled.

'Arre yaar, that Lata Sinha…'

That very same Lata Sinha.

She was twenty-four then. Dusky. Tall. Big shining eyes, sculpted hair…

The shadow of her hair
Tiptoed into my room
In the dead of night
And made a promise to be true.

The lips
That planted burning flames
On my breast and my face.
The deep eyes
That I closed silently with my lips.
The stone that sat in my heart dreaming of
 our home.
Those eyelids, the hair, the lips, the eyes –
That flawless, beautiful idol of stone
She forgot her promise.
In my room,
Alone,
I try to distract myself with playful dreams
The perfume of her body
Spreads like dishevelled hair
Appears wrapped in a soiled cloak of memories
And rises, tired of sitting in this chair for so
 long
Then sits down again and begins to weep.

Story over. Game over.

Ali Amjad remembered Lata Sinha, as if by heart ... Like his own name. Like other people's beautiful couplets. He had sung her softly. But the biggest problem with other people's poetry was that you could only sing it. You couldn't make it your own. You could only feel sad wondering why it wasn't yours.

Ali Amjad had no complaints against Lata Sinha. The tragedy was that she was Kanta Sinha's elder sister, and if she married a Muslim it would be difficult to get Kanta married … There are so many rough, difficult paths around the heart!

And these little paths turn into chains and tightly bind any dreams that dare to come near.

Ali Amjad was prepared to wait until Kanta got married. But next to Lata's heart wound the narrow little road that belonged to her widowed mother, and she was not willing to get her younger daughter married before the older one.

Lata Sinha was not unfaithful to Ali Amjad. She just suppressed her heart's desires and married Shri B.K. Srivastava, IAS. And desolation settled on Ali Amjad's heart.

> Come, for the lonely heart is now just that, a
> lonely heart
> And now, there's no sound of its beating either

'There's a Muslim too, isn't there?' Harish asked.

'Yes,' he said. 'Kishwar.'

'That's a beautiful name ... So the story is, she's middle-class. The father is a lawyer...'

'No,' Ali Amjad said. 'Kishwar's father teaches logic. Because the boy loves the girl and the girl loves the boy, it proves that love is never a good thing...'

'What?' Harish was flummoxed. 'What logic is this?'

'It doesn't matter what logic it is, the two don't get married,' Ali Amjad said.

'Why are we interested in marriage? Though let's say the marriage does take place. But the consummation doesn't happen. He is just lifting her veil when the rioters come in. They kill the husband and twenty-four men stand in line to rape the wife.'

'But why? There was no riot. Yes, she did marry someone else. Her husband has a good, respectable name. Muhammad Abdullah Khan, civil engineer, Moradabad.'

'Moradabad!' Harish said. 'No, yaar, not Moradabad, Shahjahanpur. Are you thinking of something else?'

'No. But her name was Kishwar. She was from Allahabad and she married a civil engineer from

Moradabad, Muhammad Abdullah Khan. And…' He fell silent.

'And what?'

'And I was alone once again.'

The room was quiet. And after a while, Ali Amjad left Harish alone in the silence of that room and went away. He wanted to sit by himself somewhere, and sort out his life's accounts.

VD, Alimullah, Harish…

Ruqaiya, Sabiha, Kishwar, Lata Sinha…

Bholanath, Rama Chopra, Mrs Varma, Peter aka Ramnath, the writer…

Ali Amjad found himself quite alone in this dense forest of names … It's the same for everyone. In this forest of names, everyone stares in terror at their own reflections in the broken mirrors of their individuality, reflections that are like thousand-headed monsters. There is no tomorrow. Everyone looks at their present fearfully, with their backs against the wall of yesterday. As if there is no truth left except for what has passed.

For a long time, Ali Amjad wandered without purpose in the forest of names. And kept thinking – what is the difference between living and not living … All around him, Bombay and its bustling streets remained unaware, unmindful of this question.

Bombay!
Come,
Let's go, the two of us
To the village of slumber
In this city of fog, all shadows are asleep.
Dashed on the shore of this deep sea of sweat
All respite is asleep.
The din has dimmed.
All laughter is asleep.
That soft weeping is asleep.
– All whispers are asleep.
The roads,
As they travel,
Have dissolved into houses.
The city is left standing alone.
Why don't we take this lonely, lost city with us,
To the village of slumber.
Night falls.
The eyes begin to burn.
The words are exhausted by the burden of
their voice.

SCENE: 75

Come,
Let's cover ourselves with a cloak of whispers
Come, these whispers will sustain us on our
journey.

But for Ali Amjad, there were no whispers. There was no one to go with him to the village of slumber ... The roads were awake. On the other side of the parapet, the sea was awake. The lights in the big, grand buildings were awake ... The BEST buses were awake ... Only Mai's Adda was asleep ... Because a social welfare office had opened there now. And offices shut in the evening. Mr and Mrs D'Souza had returned to Mangalore...

That night, he found out that the agony-filled stories of some beggars had sparked Hindu–Muslim tensions in some parts of the city. There had been a couple of riots ... And VD had been killed.

Ali Amjad remembered Ghalib.

It's the world that has killed you, Asadullah Khan!

If VD hadn't died like this, his death wouldn't have been suitably dramatic. God knows who would stay in that room in D'Cruz now. The story of the first dervish had ended. The remaining three awaited their turn.

Mirza Ghalib had written a letter to Hargopal Tafta:

'Look at me, I'm neither free, nor imprisoned ... Not happy, not unhappy. Not a corpse, not alive. I just keep on living. I keep on talking. I eat rotis every day. I keep drinking alcohol repeatedly. When death comes, I will die. Without gratitude. Without grievance...'

VD could have written this letter. Harish could have written this letter. Ali Amjad could also have written it...

If there is an ode to the night, sing
For this morning
Has no song
No voice
No rising sun
No sinking moon
Facing
The forest of night
Confused
Distressed
We stand...
Every single road sits holding its breath
But no one comes bringing any sign of hope
And falling on the stony surface of hard
circumstance

SCENE: 75

Laughter, like glass,
Delicate like my heart,
That laughter shatters.
Courage lies vanquished
In the eyes that have been awake all night
In the eyes that yearn for morning
There are only the embers of burnt-out moments
A nameless ache.

'The language is a little difficult,' Harish said. 'People won't understand.'

'Which people?' Ali Amjad asked. 'The people who killed VD?'

'No,' Harish said. 'VD was killed by educated people. The scene in which VD was killed was written by me, and you wrote the dialogues.'

They had been hiding this thought from themselves for the last ten or twelve days. And perhaps he'd written this poem to throw dust into his own eyes. That's why he was irritated.

'I didn't write this scene and you didn't write the dialogue,' he said. 'VD made us write it and paid us for it.' Ali Amjad was angered by his own words.

Harish poured whatever remained of the whisky into his glass.

'Screw VD and the remaining money. Drink the whisky.'

Ali Amjad drank it up and the delicious, bitter heat of the neat whisky ran through his entire body. More than the intoxication, he liked the warm, tingly feeling. That's why he never added water or soda to his drink ... Everything else was adulterated anyway. From milk to politics, there was nothing unadulterated in the market. You couldn't depend on the whisky either. The bottles were real, the alcohol was not ... So what did one get by mixing it with water or soda?

'So this proves that there's nothing to Marxism.'

Ali Amjad was startled. God knows how Harish had come to this conclusion. But he didn't want it to seem as if the remark had not registered with him. That's why, with a cigarette dangling from his lips and hunting for a match, he said:

'Why is Marxism to blame?'

'It's to blame because we are no better than those we give speeches against. At one time, VD was the secretary of the district committee. He was a leader of the Student

Federation. He was in love with Bilqis Bukhari, and he died while running a begging racket.'

'Bilqis Bukhari used to be a celebrity,' Ali Amjad said. 'She was interested in me as well for a few days. What a girl she was, by god! Everyone knew that she belonged to no one. But everyone danced to her tune. She brought a lot of boys to the Student Federation.'

'You too?'

'No. I had come a little earlier.'

'She's the one who brought me.'

'How long did it take you to find out that...'

'She was a bloody flirt.'

'But she was so interesting. When she lay down in bed beside you, it was as if a cool morning breeze was lying next to you...'

They stopped talking about VD. They began talking about Bilqis Bukhari ... And by the time the second bottle was half empty, both of them had forgotten that they'd been drinking to forget their sorrow over VD's death.

But you can't really forget sorrow! Sorrow is a reality. Like life. Or perhaps like death. And there are different kinds of deaths. VD's death was one kind. And there is another death, the kind that Ali Amjad and Harish thought was their life. The death of Mai's Adda was also a death ... And then there is the death of all those good stories that are sold and bought to be made into bad Hindi films, in some Famous Mahalaxmi office, or in the impersonal drawing-room of some Pali Hill or Juhu-Parle Scheme bungalow.

Death.
Tired of the day by evening
My heart sank like the sun.
Death.
My pain comes in wave after wave.
And hope is like a bandage, fastened tight.
The hands of time are freezing.
The sky is empty,
No sun,
Nor moon.
Moonlight like the frigid melancholy of my eyes.
Sunlight like the weariness of my face
Someone else's rhythm in the beating of my heart.
And she,
Faceless,

Formless.

No sunlight in the courtyard of my heart.

Ali Amjad came home.

VDs keep dying all the time. He had a scene to write.

Beyond the bars of the window, on the other side of the grille, the moon had descended and paused at the cluster of coconut trees ... The room was filled with the silence of the night.

Bholanath Khatak and Rama had stopped fighting.

Ali Amjad began to write again.

The very same 'Scene: 75'. The same post office. The same street munshi. The same Abulkhair's mother and the same letter.

ABULKHAIR'S MOTHER: ... And Abulkhair's father should know that everything is all right here. For two months, every evening I have been getting a slight fever. Abulkhair's older son has the black cough. The younger one has the pox. His wife has some illness. Don't know what it is. Abulkhair was hit by a taxi. His leg is broken in two places. It's in a plaster cast. Hope everything is all right there too.

The street munshi smiles.

MUNSHI: Everyone is unwell. Why are you making me say that everything is all right?

Raja's voice can be heard.

RAJA: All right now means that they are alive, they haven't died yet.

The street munshi looks sadly in Raja's direction.

MUNSHI: When I sat at the post office to write letters, I found out that there is much sorrow in our country.

RAJA: Speak softly. Otherwise they'll tax our bloody sorrows too...

Ali Amjad stopped writing. He read the last line many times...

Then he crossed it out. He wrote another line in its place.

RAJA: At least there's an excess of something in our country.

He crossed this out too. He wrote a third line.

RAJA: Arre, happiness and sorrow are all a game of destiny, street munshi. You write the bloody letter and take your twenty-five paise.

This didn't work either. He wrote a fourth line.

RAJA: You're a bloody street munshi, not a god. You're writing a bloody letter, not someone's bloody destiny.

The street munshi looks at Raja, then puts Abulkhair's mother's letter in an envelope and seals it with spit.

CUT

The scene was done.

It was still night. The silence inside the room and in the night outside remained the same. The cluster of coconut trees was silent. The old ruined fort was silent.

Ali Amjad read 'Scene: 75'. He read the lines he had crossed out. He then took a fresh sheet and began writing a fair copy of the scene ... And so, a scene without anything crossed out was finally on paper.

Destiny, it turned out, was at the root of the affair. Who can fight against destiny? Abulkhair's mother?

Everyone at home is unwell, but she'll keep writing to Abulkhair's father that everything is all right here and, Allah willing, everything is all right there too…

The pen is in the street munshi's hand and the letter is being dictated by Abulkhair's mother.

Ali Amjad put 'Scene: 75' into a file. The nocturnal silence became even more pronounced. He felt as if the sea was beating against the walls of the room and VD was sitting in the chair in front of him, smiling…

Ali Amjad felt a long yawn coming. He swallowed two tablets of Calmpose with a glass of cold water and lay down in his lonely bed.

His neighbours had stopped fighting. Rama was laughing at something. Khatakji was playing out a love scene with his wife, and outside the room the night was nearing its end.

Ali Amjad closed his eyes … When he still couldn't sleep, he took two more tablets of Calmpose. He wanted to sleep soundly because it was the premiere of his first big film the next day…

Dissolve

THE NEWS of Ali Amjad's death did not appear in any newspaper because, just like his life, he didn't choose a good time to die. To die at 3.30 in the morning is the height of foolishness. You can't even get space in the 'Stop Press' section.

Around 3.30, his servant Fernandez felt as if somebody was calling him. He took a little time to get out of bed. By the time he did, the sound had stopped. He went back to sleep.

When he went to Ali Amjad's room with a cup of tea at 10.30 in the morning, he found that Ali Amjad had fallen off the bed and was lying on the ground.

If it had been anyone else instead of Fernandez, he would have panicked. But Fernandez was a sensible man. Perry Mason. Carter Brown, Agatha Christie, Ian Fleming, Peter Cheyney ... He had read all the writers whose stories Ali Amjad, and many other writers who'd become famous, had stolen. Fernandez was actually a Mangalorean. But because he was working in a Hindi writer's house, he had developed a taste for books and literature. Often, while serving tea in the morning or dinner in the evening, he would narrate an idea or two to his sahib. Every story would begin like this: 'Sahib, I couldn't sleep at night. So, I got an idea ... It's totally original, this idea...' Ali Amjad would listen quietly. And that's why Fernandez loved Ali Amjad. Phanda Patialvi, Ramnath Banarasi and Kamal Amrohi had all tried to lure him, but he hadn't fallen into their trap. 'In all of Bombay, in all of the bloody world, I've never met a more loving sahib than him...' He was willing to accept a job which gave him 110 rupees a month. But he was not prepared to leave his sahib.

Ramnath Banarasi had acquired a Mercedes car and a twenty-four-year-old private secretary – who knew no Urdu or Hindi. But Ramnath, aka Peter, Banarasi himself knew only passable Hindi and Urdu. Fernandez liked the secretary. If he had teamed up with Ramnath Banarasi, maybe he too would have a car and a secretary. Phandaji had offered him a salary of 1,000 rupees a month, but Phandaji didn't have his sahib's qualities.

He did the novena for Ali Amjad in Mount Mary and Mahim church. Every Sunday, he would light a candle, narrate his stories, and when Ali Amjad would finally smile, Fernandez would feel as if he'd found some meaning in life…

That's why when Fernandez saw that Ali Amjad had left him, at first he couldn't believe that his sahib was capable of such disloyalty. He wanted to shake him and ask him why he'd betrayed him like this. But he had read Chase, Perry Mason and Christie. That's why he didn't touch anything in the room.

He sat down in the kitchen and began to weep. He had read in crime novels that he should first call the police. But in the Perry Mason novels, the first phone call was made to Perry Mason. Who was Perry Mason in this case? VD was dead. Alimullah didn't have a phone. That left Harish, whose film *Palkon ki Chhaon,* which was ready for its premiere, had been lifted from a Perry Mason novel, *The Case of the Crooked Nose*.

So Fernandez phoned Harish. 'Saab! Sahib is no more. He's dead!'

Harish was stunned. The naked girl lying in his bed lit a cigarette. She was new. A side heroine in one of Harish's ongoing films.

Harish looked at her. His eyes roamed over her naked body. He remembered afresh the pleasures of the night past.

'Shall I call the police, saab?' Fernandez was asking.

'No,' Harish said. 'I'll call the police. And I'll come over right away.'

The conversation ended there.

Harish was in a quandary. If news of Ali Amjad's death spread, his premiere would be ruined.

'Come no, darling,' said the naked girl who, after waking up, had, god knows how many times, in her heart of hearts, already become a big heroine like Hema Malini...

Harish didn't answer. He was worried about the premiere.

Ali Amjad was his friend.

He called his assistant director, Jog. 'Yaar, Jog saab, there's a big problem.'

'Did she turn out to be married?' Jog asked.

Harish laughed.

'No, it's not that.'

'Then what is it? And by the way, can I get two more invitations for the premiere?'

'I'm afraid the premiere may not happen at all.'

'Why?' the naked girl asked.

'Oh, shut up.'

'What?' Jog asked.

'Yaar, when will these girls get some brains?'

'No hope,' Jog said. 'If girls had brains, the government could've saved all the money it has spent on family planning.' Jog laughed at his own joke.

'Remember, I had introduced you to Ali Amjad?'

'The writer?'

'Yes.'

'Yes, yes, I remember, a most entertaining chap.'

'The problem has to do with him,' Harish said. 'The premiere is today. And he's just died. I don't know what to do.'

'How did he die?'

'I don't know. I'm going there now.'

'Where are you going?' the naked girl asked.

'I'll come too,' Jog said.

'I'll reach in half an hour. I haven't even shaved yet.'

Harish went straight to the bathroom. Stepping out of the house only after he'd shaved was his number one principle in life. He had no others.

He knew that he would have to give some sort of statement on Ali Amjad's death. And once he left the house, he wouldn't have the time to think. This too he knew very well.

Gazing into the mirror, he tried out a sad expression. He didn't like his sad face. He tried to make just his eyes look a little more sorrowful...

Ali Amjad didn't die, he was killed. And he was killed by our uncaring society, cruel circumstances and this heartless film industry...

He jerked his neck. He didn't like the statement.

My friend Ali Amjad lived like a man and died like a Hindi film – without reason...

As he shaved, he mentally prepared his statement. And so, when he entered Ali Amjad's flat, he was not worried in the least.

Fernandez was crying.

Then Jog arrived. Harish went with him to Ali Amjad's bedroom.

Ali Amjad was lying on the floor next to the bed.

'He's dead,' Jog said.

Harish looked at Ali Amjad's corpse.

'Don't worry,' Jog said. 'I'll make sure there's no post-mortem.'

'No,' Harish said. 'Friendship has its place, the law has its place. There must be a post-mortem.'

SCENE: 75

Harish was worried that if there was no post-mortem, Ali Amjad's burial would clash with his premiere, and he didn't want to miss Ali Amjad's burial. 'After all, this is my friend's dead body.' To himself, he said, 'What's more, Ali Amjad would never have wanted the premiere of *Palkon ki Chhaon* to be cancelled because of him, given that Gujral sahib is coming down from Delhi especially for it ... And after the premiere, there are cocktails at the Taj Intercontinental.'

'As you wish,' Jog said. 'Where's the phone?'

'In the kitchen.'

Jog went off to call for an ambulance. And when the ambulance came, the residents of Sursingar discovered that Ali Amjad had died.

Rama Chopra immediately got down to working the phone. The first call was to Mrs Midha. 'Listen to this, Ali Amjad died. Yes. Last night.' And then she started crying for real.

Rama was crying for Ali Amjad, Ali Amjad who meant nothing to her. 'Hai, poor thing. He was such a good boy...'

Wrapped in a towel, Khatakji emerged from the bathroom. He interrupted Rama and dialled Manchandani, 'Hello.'

'Hello,' said Manchandani from the other side.

'Your tenant died last night.'

'What? How did he die?'

'Never mind how he died. I want that flat. If you want to sell it, sell it. If you want to give it on rent, that's okay too. If you want key money, let me know ... All right. No, not in the evening. We'll have to go for the burial in the evening. Let's meet tomorrow morning...'

'Do you have no shame?' Rama said. 'That poor man is lying dead and you're talking about flats!'

'Why are you so sad at his death?'

'He was my lover, no...'

'Who knows, he might have been...'

The phone rang. Suddenly Khatakji became Bholanath.

'Hello,' he said lovingly.

'This is Ramnath Banarasi speaking. What is this I'm hearing about Ali Amjad...'

'Why don't you come out of your flat and see for yourself?' From Bholanath, he became Khatakji again. He said to Rama, 'I don't want any crying-shying in this house because of that harami da puttar...'

He went out, still wrapped in his towel. A lot of people from the building society were standing around. In the fifteen-year history of Sursingar Cooperative Housing Society Private Limited, this was the first instance of suicide, murder, or perhaps even straightforward death.

Seeing so many people, Khatakji rushed back into his flat. He put on a brick-coloured shirt, olive bell bottoms, and holding a 555 cigarette, he went out again.

Everyone was still standing around in the same place as before. They were talking about how someone or the other from Ali Amjad's home was sure to turn up. The carpet was rather nice. Many people had their eye on it.

Rama was shedding real tears inside when talk about the carpet reached her ears. She opened the door and looked at everyone, her eyes red from crying.

'I'd spoken about that carpet with bhai sahib just two days ago, and he said that he wouldn't take any money from his sister. But I insisted that I would pay him. We settled at 800.'

Khatakji said, 'The late Ali Amjad was so fond of Rama. What a man he was, sahib! He didn't seem like a Muslim at all ... Just a few days ago, I praised the cut-glass vase in his drawing room. Bas, he told me to take it ... I kept refusing. But he was adamant. So I said, all right, I'll take it on my birthday.'

'That bloody vase broke when it slipped from my hands,' Fernandez said, wiping his tears. 'It's been more than two months now.'

Apart from Mrs Varma, nobody looked at Khatak. But everyone fell silent. At exactly that moment, Jog came out of the flat, followed by the attendants carrying Ali Amjad's body on a stretcher. They passed through the throng of Sursingar's residents. Then Harish came out of the flat.

'Fernandez, look after the house. We won't get the body back before tomorrow afternoon...'

'Ji saab.'

'The burial will only take place tomorrow evening.'

'Ji saab.'

'I tried hard that there should be no post-mortem,' Harish said to the society residents. 'Jog is my friend. But he can't put his job at risk. He said that the deceased was a well-known person. You can't hide the news of his suicide.'

'Suicide?' Several people spoke up at the same time.

Harish thought it best not to reply. Shrugging his shoulders, he quickly went down the stairs to the street.

Before him, the sea was still, as if waiting. Two or three children were running around. Harish's Nova was parked there, the sea reflected in its gleaming red polish. He was free of Ali Amjad.

And all of a sudden, thoughts of the premiere of *Palkon ki Chhaon* overtook him. God knows if Yusuf sahib would come or not. It had been decided that Dilip Kumar would introduce the unit of *Palkon ki Chhaon* to the guests. He would also have to take care of Dharmendra, Rajesh Khanna and Amitabh Bachchan. Dharmendra was a simple soul. Genial. Not the sort who got annoyed or upset easily. Amitabh was also not a problem. But Rajesh Khanna? He had an inferiority complex...

Harish started the car.

The premiere was at nine o'clock.

Crowds started gathering at seven. First came the police. Then the rest of the people. They started surrounding the cars of stars they recognized ... A taxi stopped. Khatak and Mrs Khatak. Khatakji was in a suit, and on Rama's neck glittered a diamond pendant that she had especially borrowed from Mrs Midha for this occasion. Mr Varma didn't come. Mrs Varma didn't come. Tolaram, the broker, came with his secretary. Ramnath Banarasi was there. Pancharan Mishra was there. Alimullah was there ... All those people who had wangled invitation cards for the premiere from Ali Amjad had turned up…

The hall was packed to the rafters. Only one chair was empty. But in that crowd and chaos, nobody paid any attention to that vacant chair. That chair was meant for the film's scriptwriter, Sayyid Ali Amjad Husaini Tirmizi Barabankvi.

'I can't see Ali Amjad anywhere,' Alimullah said to Harish at the cocktail party.

'Yes,' Harish said. 'He died sometime last night.' As he spoke, he suddenly smiled because a photographer was taking a picture of him with Hema Malini, who happened to be standing nearby.

FADE OUT

P.S.

Insights,
Interviews
&
More …

Rahi Masoom Raza: Ek Hindustani

Poonam Saxena

The first thing I read when I opened *Scene: 75* was the 'Vasiyat' ('Will and Testament'). I was so moved, I kept going back to it until, finally, I took a picture and pasted it on my laptop screen so that I could see it every time I opened my computer. At that time, all I knew about Rahi Masoom Raza was that he was a highly respected poet and novelist, though his success as a writer of Hindi films had somewhat overshadowed his literary accomplishments. But what eventually eclipsed everything – at least in the popular imagination – was that he was the writer of the majestic dialogues for the blockbuster TV series *Mahabharat*. Over time, as I read more and more about him and his life, I realized that the 'Vasiyat' was a true mirror of the kind of man he was: an unsparing critic of fundamentalists and hypocrites of every hue, with deep roots in his hometown in Ghazipur, Uttar Pradesh. All this found reflection in his writing, which also had a strong dose of biting humour that made you laugh out loud and wince at once.

Scene: 75 itself is a darkly funny, surreal novel in which Rahi sahib casts an unsparing, satirical look at the Hindi film industry of the 1970s and also writes about Hindu–Muslim relations with his customary blistering honesty. The book begins with Ali Amjad, a struggling scriptwriter from Benares, trapped in a lonely Bombay flat, and ends with him still trapped in that lonely flat. But in the middle is a teeming, intertwined, untidy throng of cynical and manipulative characters and their equally fantastic stories, narrated with a no-holds-barred candour by Rahi sahib. Unscrupulous film producers and ambitious clerks rub shoulders with wealthy lesbians and bigoted middle-class social climbers. There are few lovable characters. When I finished the novel, I realized that the only character I cared for was Ali Amjad (Rahi sahib himself, I think) – nevertheless, all of them held my undivided interest. They made me laugh even as I shook my head in disbelief at their doings.

Rahi sahib wrote several novels between 1966 and 1986, the best-known of which is the first one, *Aadha Gaon*, a vivid, true-to-life depiction of the Shia community in a village, Gangauli, in the United Provinces at the time of Partition. The lives of Muslims in India and their relationship with Hindus formed the central motif in many of Rahi sahib's works, including the brilliant *Topi Shukla* (1968) and *Os Ki Boond* (1970). Even in *Scene: 75*, this fraught relationship is thrown into sharp focus. Ali Amjad is hunting for a house and can't find one because he is a Muslim. He is asked to pretend he's a Sindhi by a prospective landlord, but Ali Amjad refuses:

> 'I am a Muslim and I also work in films,' Ali Amjad said. He thought it was necessary for him to say this. He was not a religious man. He didn't believe in Allah. He didn't do namaz. He didn't fast during Ramzan. He was an uncompromising critic of organizations like the Muslim League and the Jamat-e-Islami ... But he was not ashamed of the fact that he had been born into a Muslim family. And he did not want to insult himself or his country by hiding his name and identity.

Ali Amjad meets people who openly tell him that they have no love for Muslims – like Rama Chopra, his neighbour in the housing society where he finally manages to rent a flat. Partition has created a cloud of hate and lies in the minds of people like Rama:

> Hating Muslims had become a sort of fashion in north India in those days. Everyone had the number of people killed in Pakistan on their fingertips, and they were so preoccupied with this arithmetic that they had no time to count the corpses lying on the streets of Hindustan. They believed that only Hindu women had honour and Muslim women just had bodies. But even in those days, there were a few crazy people here and there, on both sides of the border, who screamed themselves hoarse saying that dead bodies and daggers had no religion, and honour had no identity or caste. But Rama didn't have even one such crazy person as her neighbour. That's why no one told Rama that Muslims in India had been killed, just like Hindus in Pakistan.

But unlike his other novels, *Scene: 75* is not so sharply focused on Hindu–Muslim relations. Three of Rahi sahib's novels feature the Hindi film industry – *Himmat Jaunpuri* (1969), *Dil Ek Sada Kagaz* (1973) and of course *Scene: 75* (1977). Despite my best efforts, I have not been able to get a copy of *Himmat Jaunpuri*. (I have been told it is out of print.) *Dil Ek Sada Kagaz*, the story of Raffan, is set in three different milieus, and the Bombay film industry is just one of them. But *Scene: 75* is set wholly in the city's movie world. Here Rahi sahib rips off the tinsel curtain that hides the film industry's, insecurity and desperation for success. He spares no one – not even the young men from small towns engaged in their perilous journey of surviving in a big, impersonal city. The novel has been cast in the shade by Rahi sahib's weightier works like *Aadha Gaon* and *Topi Shukla*, but it is remarkable for its kaleidoscope-like structure of stories within stories, its black humour and its sharp social commentary.

Rahi sahib came to Bombay in 1967 to try his luck in Hindi films, and lived and worked there until his death in 1992. He wrote the script and dialogues for over 300 films, including enduring hits such as *Mili* (1975), *Main Tulsi Tere Aangan Ki* (1978), *Gol Maal* (1979), *Karz* (1980), *Lamhe* (1991) and many others. But he is best remembered for his dialogues for the 94-episode mega TV series, *Mahabharat*, in the late 1980s. There's an interesting story about how Rahi sahib took up this challenging project. According to his close friend and colleague at Aligarh Muslim

University (AMU), Kunwarpal Singh,[1] when film-maker B.R. Chopra requested Rahi sahib to write the dialogues, he declined, saying he didn't have the time. But B.R. Chopra went ahead and announced Rahi sahib's name at a press conference anyway. In no time, letters of opposition from self-styled protectors of the Hindu faith arrived: Were all Hindus dead that Chopra had to give this task to a Muslim? Chopra promptly forwarded the letters to Rahi sahib. Ever the champion of India's syncretic culture, Rahi sahib called Chopra the next day and said, 'Chopra sahib! I will write the *Mahabharat*. I am a son of the Ganga. Who knows the civilization and culture of India better than I do?'

In an interview with *India Today* magazine in 1990, when he was asked about the opposition from Hindu fundamentalist groups, he answered: 'I'm hurt and amazed at the furore created about a Muslim writing the script. Am I not an Indian?'[2]

These words came from Rahi sahib's heart. He always identified himself as a Ganga-putra, a Ganga-kinare-wala.

---

[1] *Rahi Masoom Raza* by Kunwarpal Singh (Sahitya Akademi, 2005). Some of the information in this essay is from this 96-page monograph.

[2] http://indiatoday.intoday.in/story/mahabharat-can-easily-contend-to-be-the-most-powerful-story-of-the-world-rahi-masoom-raza/1/314815.html

He was born in 1927 in Ghazipur in eastern Uttar Pradesh, on the banks of the Ganga, and retained a deep attachment to his childhood home all his life. (Poet and lyricist Javed Akhtar said in an interview that Rahi sahib found a way to introduce his hometown into every conversation, even if it was about the United Nations Security Council.)[3]

His father was a well-known lawyer and he grew up in a big, sprawling, prosperous home. (Zaidi Villa of *Dil Ek Sada Kagaz* is said to have echoes of this haveli.) He was the second of four brothers. His elder brother, Moonis Raza, had an illustrious career in public life: he was, among other things, Founder–Chairman of the Jawaharlal Nehru University and Vice Chancellor of Delhi University. After Rahi sahib came Mehndi Raza who became head of the geography department in AMU, and the fourth brother was the economist Ahmad Raza who worked with the IMF in Washington. Rahi sahib had five sisters, of whom the youngest, Suraiya, went on to do an MA and a PhD in history with the support of Moonis Raza and Rahi sahib, despite opposition from the family.

Rahi sahib was a sickly child. At the age of eleven, he contracted tuberculosis and spent five years in the salubrious environs of Bhowali (in Nainital district), recovering from the illness. He returned to Ghazipur in

---

[3] http://fwa.co.in/ogtemplate.php?get=FWAoig6

1942 and resumed his education. But after he finished high school, he was struck with the disease again, and this time he went to Kashmir to recuperate.

After he came back, an interesting incident took place. Pabbar Ram, a communist candidate, decided to contest the elections for the post of chairman, Municipal Board of Ghazipur. By then, Moonis Raza was quite active in the Communist Party and Rahi sahib had followed suit. It so happened that Pabbar Ram's chief opponent was Bashir Hasan Abadi, Moonis and Rahi Masoom Raza's father. The brothers were in a quandary. They went and spoke to their father who declared that he had been a disciplined Congress man since 1930 and wasn't about to flout the party's decision now. But Rahi sahib and Moonis Raza went ahead and supported Pabbar Ram and he ended up winning the election. (What Bashir Hasan Abadi thought of this is not recorded.)

After finishing his school education in Ghazipur, Rahi sahib went to Aligarh for higher studies and did a doctorate in Hindustani literature. By the early 1960s, he had got a job as an Urdu lecturer in AMU. Javed Akhtar, in an interview, says, 'Rahi sahib was a cult figure [on the campus]. He enjoyed a huge fan-following among the students, boys and girls both, owing to his charming and stylish persona. His admirers would walk by his side whenever he roamed [around] in the campus. He would limp a bit, for he had been affected by polio in his childhood, but his elegant sherwani, which he would never button, and the classy kurta, would make it clear that he was no ordinary man. He was a star.'[4] Rahi sahib's nephew, the Lucknow-based writer and scholar Nadeem Hasnain, says that after the Urdu poet Majaz, it was only Rahi sahib who enjoyed such widespread popularity on the AMU campus. 'It was said that the AMU girls kept his photograph under their pillows,' he says.[5] (When he came to Bombay, Rahi sahib was advised to change his style of dressing to suit a modern metropolis. But he stuck to his cream-coloured sherwanis, angarkhas

---

[4] Ibid.

[5] In the same interview (http://www.youtube.com/watch?v=127b3uSywjs), Nadeem Hasnain says that before Rahi sahib began writing in earnest, he used to dash off romantic novels for the very popular *Rumani Duniya*, published by the Allahabad-based Nikhat Publications, under the pen name of Shahid Akhtar. Along with *Rumani Duniya*, the publishing house also brought out *Jasoosi Duniya* and the star writer of those novels was Ibn Safi. But when Ibn Safi became unwell, Rahi sahib was pressed into service and he began contributing to *Jasoosi Duniya* as well. Hasnain remembers seeing Rahi sahib in Ghazipur, writing two or three novels simultaneously on different clipboards!

and Aligarhi pyjamas. Indeed, that became his unique sartorial statement.) Photographs of the young Rahi show a dashing-looking man with an irresistible smile – it's not hard to see why the girls were crazy about him.

If things were going so swimmingly in Aligarh, why did he uproot himself and shift to Bombay? According to Kunwarpal Singh, this decision was triggered by his wedding to Nayyar Jahan in 1965. She had been previously married, but Rahi sahib fell in love with her and, despite opposition, went ahead and made her his wife. A full-blown scandal erupted and Rahi sahib lost his job at AMU (though Kunwarpal Singh says that the scandal merely gave his rivals and foes an excuse: they had always been opposed to his attempts to introduce Hindi courses in the Urdu department and vice versa).

Aadha Gaon had been published by then. It had brought him renown but was of no help in securing a livelihood. Nadeem Khan, Rahi sahib's son, says that it was film-maker Ramesh Chandra, an Aligarh acquaintance of Rahi sahib's (also the older brother of actor Bharat Bhushan), who invited him to come to Bombay and try his luck in the film industry.[6]

---

[6] This and other quotes from Nadeem Khan are from a personal interview conducted on 9 October 2017.

And that's what he did. Initially, there was no work. He tided over that difficult period with the help of his writer friends like Kamleshwar (who was editing the magazine *Sarika* then) and Dharamvir Bharati (who was editing *Dharmyug*). His writings were published in their magazines; often they paid him in advance. But slowly, he began establishing himself in the film industry. He worked closely with film-makers such as Raj Khosla, B.R. Chopra, Yash Chopra, Hrishikesh Mukherjee and others. He became acquainted with the art of writing dialogues. Kunwarpal Singh recounts how once Rahi sahib had to write the dialogues for a Raj Khosla film. When the latter came to read the script, he kept saying, 'Kya baat hai! Bahut khoob!' as he turned the pages. At the same time, he kept cutting the dialogues. In the end, he kept just two or three lines out of every two pages. Rahi sahib learnt his lesson – in cinema, you don't need verbosity; pages of dialogue can sometimes be communicated through a single close-up on screen. Over time, he became a consummate practitioner, winning two Filmfare Awards for Best Dialogue (for *Main Tulsi Tere Aangan Ki* and *Mili*).

Nadeem Khan remembers how he got his third award. Rahi sahib had written the dialogues for *Lamhe* and was very disappointed when it performed poorly at the box-office. He was proud of the work he had done in the film and had hoped for a Filmfare Award. But soon after *Lamhe* released, he passed away. He was just 65. Not long after that, Nadeem Khan, who was then working as the cinematographer for a Rakesh Roshan film, *King Uncle*, got a call from *Filmfare*. Rahi sahib had won the Best Dialogue Award for *Lamhe* posthumously. Khan remembers going to the function and collecting the award on his behalf. Jeetendra, the actor, was on stage and started crying. Khan says he felt his eyes welling up too. 'As I came down, there was B.R. Chopra on one side and Yash Chopra on the other. Both kept hugging me,' he recalls. 'I went home and put the award in front of Rahi sahib's photograph.'

The masterful dialogues for *Mahabharat* and the decision to make Samay (Time) the narrator were what elevated the series to another plane. The production values and acting left much to be desired, but the powerful dialogues by Rahi sahib made the show the astounding success that it was. He coined new words, such as 'Pitashri' and 'Matashri', which became so popular that people thought this was how characters must have spoken in ancient times. The truth is that Rahi sahib adapted these words from the way family members are addressed in Urdu – 'Ammijaan', 'Abbajaan' and so on.

Nadeem Khan says that those years of writing the *Mahabharat* took their toll on Rahi sahib: 'He aged fifteen years in that time. It was very stressful – he couldn't afford to take one wrong step,' he says. 'After *Mahabharat*, he was supposed to write another TV show, *Om Namah Shivay* (he was a great Shiv bhakt). But that was not to be.'

After the triumph of *Mahabharat*, Khan says he urged Rahi sahib to charge a higher fee for his work. But he refused. 'He would say, "This is my home, the door is always open." And indeed, the door of the house was always open. "Every day ten or fifteen people drop in, dastarkhwaan lagta hai, what more do I want?"' says Khan. He was known to write films for free – and sometimes just for a paan that the producer would bring him!

He wrote his scripts during the day, sitting in his living room on the carpet, with the noise of the household around him. But his books he would write in the dead of night.

He continued with his writing even after coming to Bombay – *Topi Shukla* came out in 1968, followed by *Himmat Jaunpuri* in 1969, and in the 1970s came *Os Ki Boond, Dil Ek Sada Kagaz, Scene: 75, Neem Ka Ped* (which was made into a TV series in 1991) and *Katra Bi Arzoo*.

While he is celebrated for his novels, he is also justly famous as a poet who could write in both Urdu and Hindi with equal felicity. He has several poetry collections to his credit, such as *Ajnabi Sheher Ke Ajnabi Raaste* and *Main Ek Pheriwala Hoon*. Some of his most admired poems find a place in *Scene: 75* ('The worlds that I am estranged from, how are they now...'). He could write romantic poetry but he was also a keen political poet, and though he never joined the Communist Party, he was clearly left-leaning. A sharp critic of the Emergency, his novel *Katra Bi Arzoo* is about those years. Hasnain, who calls Rahi sahib the 'perpetual dissenter', remembers that when Rahi sahib visited Lucknow for an event at the time, he requested his uncle to recite some poetry. Rahi sahib responded by reciting a poem that he had written on the Emergency:

> There is no leader, no road, no destination
> Nothing is harder than to just exist
> If you see a jail somewhere, stop and offer your devotion
> For there is no other place worthy of it
> There are no more gatherings in this city, Rahi
> Where wounded souls might find solace

Few people know that Rahi sahib wrote a stirring epic poem on the 1857 uprising, the first war of independence, called 'Krantikatha'. Always a champion of Hindu–Muslim unity, he was inspired by its fervent display in the 1857 uprising against the British, as also by the heroic women leaders of the movement, such as Rani Lakshmibai (there are almost forty pages dedicated to her in the poem).

> The British forced their way in, wreaked havoc
>   in every home
> And strung up nooses from every tree along
>   the roads
> At every home, at every door, a fearsome death
>   called out
> Who set the damp wood of life on fire
> While all the traitors fanned the flames?
> Listen my brothers, listen, to the story of 1857

Also not very well known is the fact that Rahi sahib wrote a book on one of India's greatest war heroes, Abdul Hamid of Ghazipur. The 1965 war with Pakistan had seen an ugly escalation of anti-Muslim feeling in the country. In an eerily familiar development, Muslims were being asked to prove their patriotism to the nation. But Y.B. Chavan, who was the defence minister then, resolved to stem this tide of communal tension and suspicion. He decided to have the story of Abdul Hamid disseminated in every possible way. During the war, Abdul Hamid had served as a havaldar in the 4th Grenadiers. In the fierce battle of Asal Utur in Punjab, he had single-handedly destroyed many Pakistani tanks, but lost his life in the process. He was awarded the Param Vir Chakra posthumously. The task of writing the book fell on Rahi sahib who got a call from the defence ministry, requesting him to undertake this project. He agreed immediately. It was published in January 1966 with a foreword by Y.B. Chavan, and was called *Chhote Aadmi Ki Badi Kahani*.

Rahi sahib wrote: 'I want to know what the great men who claim that Muslims are Pakistani spies have to say about Abdul Hamid. What do they think about his young widow Rasoolan and what have they decided about Hamid's four children? Abdul Hamid is the symbol of the Hindustani farmer and the Hindustani Musalman. He is asking a question from the battlefield. He is asking – is he a Pakistani spy?'[7]

Rahi sahib dedicated *Chhote Aadmi Ki Badi Kahani* to his nephew and niece: 'I will leave for you the traditions of a great country, Hindustan. Always be proud of the fact that you are a Hindustani … Nobody can snatch from you your right to be a Hindustani … If you meet people

---

7 *Rahi Masoom Raza* by Kunwarpal Singh (Sahitya Akademi, 2005).

who say you are not a Hindustani, know them to be liars and traitors.'[8]

Rahi sahib belonged to another world and another age – even though he lived in Bombay for many years, he never stopped longing for his beloved Ghazipur. He was symbolic of and steeped in the famed Ganga–Jamuni tehzeeb of Uttar Pradesh, which is not a myth, but a living, breathing thing. It is a milieu that is reflected in all his novels and his poetry. He was staunchly opposed to all kinds of fundamentalists, Hindu or Muslim. 'The interesting thing is, I am not a kaafir, nor am I a Musalman. I am a Hindustani Musalman and I have no other identity apart from this,' he wrote in a collection of his non-fiction writing, *Lagta Hai Bekaar Hue Hum*.

And nothing more needs to be said.

Delhi
12 October 2017

---

[8] Ibid.

A Note on the Translation

Poonam Saxena

As I discovered all the fascinating stories and incidents from Rahi sahib's life, which illustrated the kind of person he was, I also got to know *Scene: 75* very closely since – as I'm sure all translators do – I read it again and again and again. But even after several readings, I still laughed out loud at the same places, I still felt my heart grow heavy as the mood darkened, and I still grappled with difficult-to-translate sentences and words. The task became even more daunting because of Rahi sahib's carelessness with details. For example, the room in which the four friends stayed in D'Cruz Guest House changes from number five to number seven (we stayed with five, since it's mostly that). In one part of the book, we are told VD called on the phone;

and then suddenly we find VD getting up and leaving the room. So did he call or did he visit? In another part of the novel the Sursingar Cooperative Housing Society suddenly acquires another name. And so on. It was puzzling – but the only conclusion I could come to was that Rahi sahib had probably just forgotten what he'd written earlier and there was no eagle-eyed editor to catch the inconsistencies.

The task of translation was further complicated by the corkscrew character of the novel – one story begins, leads to another, which leads to another, which leads to another, and then suddenly we are back to the first story … and so on. It is like being taken through an intricate maze where, after several turns, we find that we have come back to the same place. But as a translator, I had to be careful as I walked through this maze.

But it was enjoyable and rewarding. That is the nasha of translation.

Under Rahi's Shadow

Danish Husain

Long before I was born, my life's narrative was yoked to the grand narrative of *Aadha Gaon*. As if I were some far-flung satellite fated to pirouette eternally in a corner of its massive orbit.

The story begins like this: When my father finished high school and had to join college in Ghazipur city, my grandmother took him to Bashir Manzil and requested Bashir Hasan Vakil sahib, father of Rahi Masoom Raza, to keep my father as a houseguest. And that's how *Aadha Gaon* got intricately entwined with my life.

So much so that when I read the novel in my teens, I was confused. How could one call it a work of fiction? In my head then, fiction necessarily meant something bearing no resemblance to the real world. But half the characters in this book were living, talking, real people whom I had grown up with, especially Rahi sahib's brothers and sisters – Moonis Dadda, Afsari Nanna, Sallan Dadda, Munni Dadda.

Aadha Gaon has a sense of displacement like Edward Said's memoir *Out of Place*, and a landscape like Gabriel Garcia Marquez's *One Hundred Years of Solitude*. It tears into its readers, and like an unwarranted remark finds a snug corner in their heart only to leap out unexpectedly. Like Said, Rahi sahib's characters are also perpetually on a journey to find their moral compasses and unearth their self-identities, which is invariably a walk through the minefield of the times they're living in. In some ways, all these characters speak of Rahi sahib's own quest to find his station in the constantly changing landscape of his motherland. In fact, he dedicates his novel *Scene: 75* to his three mothers: Nafisa Begum, Aligarh University and the river Ganga.

And here, when discussing the changing landscape, *Aadha Gaon* comes closer to Marquez's *One Hundred Years of Solitude*. A story of a village that loses its narrative in its telling, a story of identity lost, a story of displacement. Living as Syeds in Ghazipur, we all traced our lineage to Masood Ghazi, a medieval noble who received much of the land constituting modern Ghazipur as largesse for defeating the local chieftain Chakwa Mandhata. In some sense, similar to José Arcadio Buendía, the patriarch who founded Macondo in Marquez's novel. Though *Aadha Gaon* maps only over three decades, from the late 1930s to the 1960s, unlike Marquez's novel which is over seven generations, the template is similar – a group of people in a geographical location losing the threads of their own narratives. *Aadha Gaon* becomes a universal tale for any narrative of displacement, whether one is physically displaced or one loses one's narrative while remaining in the same place. And Rahi sahib experienced both. His moves from Gangauli to Ghazipur to Aligarh to Bombay were not fluid transitions but often painful displacements entangled in personal loss and ideological disputes.

However, the footnote here is that *Aadha Gaon* (1966) came into existence before Edward Said's *Out of Place* (1999) and Gabriel Garcia Marquez's *One Hundred Years of Solitude* (1967).

I know I am writing about *Scene: 75* and not *Aadha Gaon*, but like most great artists, Rahi sahib too picked the thread and pushed the narrative forward with each subsequent work. One may say that each work is a sub-event in the meta-event that his literary work creates, and that event is best represented in his seminal work *Aadha Gaon*.

Ali Amjad, the writer in *Scene: 75*, for example, too becomes the displaced Rahi sahib in Bombay who is trying to find his feet as he gets entangled in the stories of the characters around him. And Ali Amjad's death is the notional death of every conscientious writer in the city who compromises values to see his or her name in the credits. Rahi sahib uses his tales both as a tool for critiquing this world, and as a swan song for the dispossessed. He is unsparing, almost Manto-like, in his critique of his contemporaries and sometimes does not even spare himself as we see in *Scene: 75*, where two characters condemn him in a conversation.

That's how fluid and reality-bending Rahi sahib's literary style was. He deftly mixed the real and the imagined, and created some unforgettable narratives. His fictional characters live his real-life story as in *Dil Ek Sada Kagaz,* or characters appear bearing real names like Bilqis, my mom's namesake in *Topi Shukla*. But for all their mirroring, in the end his stories expand and consume the readers' narratives too. They are everyone's stories.

We were distant, poor cousins, and a lot of our growing up was under the extended narrative of Masoom Mamu (dad would call him 'Mamu', i.e., maternal uncle) and the tilismi world he inhabited.

There'd be days when a cryptic phone call would come in the evening. Dad would tell Mom that Mamu needed him urgently, that he was leaving for Bombay straight from the office, and could she rush a pair of spare clothes, his kurta-pajama, toothbrush and medicines to the office? He would stuff them into his office jhola and head to Bombay. And then we would wait. When Dad would return a couple of days later, he'd be dressed exactly the way he had been when he'd left for office, as if the day had stretched for seventy-two hours to fill itself with his and Masoom Mamu's stories. We would hear of some film star or the other, anecdotes from his personal life, tidbits about life in Bombay, and so on and so forth.

I recall one stark image of him filling the boot of his car with 'objectionable literature' and dumping the books at a friend's house when the Emergency was declared. In fact, he was one of the few writers who responded literarily to the Emergency with his novel *Katra Bi Aarzoo* and vociferously opposed the Film Writers Association's move to endorse the imposition. I would devour all these stories and imagine the physical spaces where they played out.

At some stage in my life I started performing stories, especially from the master epic *Dastan-e-Amir Hamza* and its sub-section *Tilism-e-Hoshruba*. Later, I discovered that Rahi sahib too had worked on *Hoshruba* and had submitted his doctoral thesis on the representation of Indian culture in the tales therein. His storytelling style at times reflects the narrative styles of oral traditions. The story tags a character and follows it, until it tags another. The plot is not paramount, it is the journey of the character that becomes the principal pursuit. We find this meandering style best in *Scene: 75*. Though it opens with Ali Amjad, it moves on to several characters around him, and then finally weaves all this back into a composite universe of Ali Amjad before ending with him. A qissagoi style, which we also see Asghar Ali Wajahat successfully deploy in his novel *Baqarganj Ke Syed*.

In fact, the physical setting for his writing was also like oral storytelling – taking detours and riddled with subplots. I recall that we stayed at his place on my first visit to Mumbai in 1983. He would write lounging on the carpet, reclining against bolsters, with a traditional writing desk in front of him, and scripts and conversations strewn all around. My grandaunt, his wife Nayyar Jahan, told me that often he would write two to three scripts simultaneously, while this melee surrounded him. He just loved the presence of his family and friends. It reminds me of an anecdote about the great dastango, Ahmed Husain Qamar, who would often dictate multiple episodes of *Tilism-e-Hoshruba* to his scribes while pacing up and down his living room and simultaneously having other conversations on the side.

It is ironic that many decades later, dispossessed and displaced, I chalk the same route and find myself in Mumbai as an actor-writer-director. My earliest memory of him is of the winter of 1980–81, when I was in the sixth grade and everyone in class disbelieved me when I said that the writer of the story 'Chhote Aadmi Ki Badi Kahani', a biographical sketch of Param Vir Chakra recipient Abdul Hameed, was my granduncle. Luckily, Rahi sahib was visiting us then. After school, I caught him basking in the winter sun on the lawn and asked him to autograph the chapter in my textbook. On hearing my ordeal at school, he laughed, signed the textbook and left me with the lesson that one doesn't need to be big to do big things.

Contrary to his fame as a film writer, we all grew up knowing him more as a literary giant and a poet. I think if Rahi sahib had not written a single film script or song, he still would have retained his place in the pantheon of twentieth-century Hindi and Urdu littérateurs. We're fortunate that he enriched Indian cinema too, and unfortunate that he went away too early.

Mumbai
7 October 2017

Acknowledgements

THANK YOU, Nadeem Khan, for sharing those wonderful stories and anecdotes about Rahi sahib.

I'm grateful to my friends Mihir Pandya and Suman Parmar for pitching in so generously and helping decipher some sentences and phrases in the text.

Athar Rather, many thanks for sitting with me and patiently going through the nuances of the Urdu in Rahi sahib's poetry.

To my fabulous editor at HarperCollins, Rahul Soni, who took so much care over the manuscript, offering excellent suggestions, even as we scratched our heads over some of the inconsistencies in Rahi sahib's text – I'm indebted to you. (And I'm happy to have introduced you to Waste!)

Danish Husain: Bahut, bahut shukriya. And a salaam to Rahi sahib, dil se.

Nadeem Hasnain sahib, thank you for your kindness and for your help with the poem 'Koi rahbar...'

To the inimitable Mita Kapur, my gratitude for always being there, for all the good and sensible advice, for pushing me when needed and giving me space when needed.

No acknowledgements can be complete without thanking Arun, who understands that there will be months when I will simply disappear behind a computer screen, oblivious to everything around me. (But I missed you, Arjun, while writing this one, though the long-distance phone conversations were – and are! – very precious.)

A heartfelt thank you to my parents, for encouraging me in all my book projects.

And to Rahi sahib, of course, for writing this sparkling little gem.

– Poonam Saxena